WEARING
THE GREEK
MILLIONAIRE'S
RING

WEARING THE GREEK MILLIONAIRE'S RING

JENNIFER FAYE

MILLS & BOON

First published in Great Britain 2019
by Mills & Boon, an imprint of HarperCollins*Publishers*
1 London Bridge Street, London, SE1 9GF

Large Print edition 2020

© 2019 Jennifer F. Stroka

ISBN: 978-0-263-08407-8

PROLOGUE

May... Infinity Island, Greece

SOMETIMES SHE FELT as though there was nowhere she truly belonged.

And sometimes she enjoyed the freedom that allowed her.

Other times, like now, Stasia Marinakos wanted a clear path in life.

She'd had one not so long ago. Suddenly, that life had been brutally wrenched from her grasp. Though with each passing day, she was learning to live with the loss, allowing herself to smile again and forcing herself to remember that she was still living and breathing.

For the almost two years since her husband passed, Stasia had been focused on fulfilling his last wishes, tending to his estate and piecing together the broken pieces of her heart. But now that was complete. All of his wishes had been fulfilled, except one.

As she sat at one of the tables at the Hideaway Café, her gaze moved across the table to her brother. She knew if she opened up to him he wouldn't understand. He would try to tell her what to do with her life and she didn't want that. She needed to find her own answers.

Xander thought she should be cautious with her money and with her life. He wasn't anxious for her to move on, which she found interesting considering he hadn't liked her husband in the beginning. In fact, Xander had vehemently disapproved of him until just before Lukos found out that he was sick—

Stasia halted her thoughts. She didn't want to go down that road. She needed to focus on the here and now. It was the only thing she could control.

"What am I supposed to do with this?"

Stasia held up a cruise ship ticket while sending her big brother a puzzled look. She didn't have time for a vacation. Now that she was on her own, with no husband and no other family besides Xander, who now had a wife and baby, she needed to pull herself together and carve out a life for herself. That had to be her priority. As it was, she'd put it off for too long.

"Use the ticket and go on vacation." Xander frowned at her as though he was concerned about her.

She shoved the ticket back across the table. "I don't have time—"

"Sure you do." Xander wasn't a man used to hearing the word *no.* "Now that our real-estate deal fell apart—of which I am sorry—you have all the time in the world." He sent her a reassuring smile. "And don't worry. By the time you get back, I'll have a new deal lined up that we can go in on together."

How did she tell him that she no longer wanted to be involved in a deal without hurting his feelings? After all, she was the one who had come up with the idea of them working together in the first place. He'd initially been resistant to the idea, but she'd kept after him until he'd finally given in.

Of course, she'd had some help getting him to change his mind—Roberto Carrass, her brother's best friend, who'd recently been elevated to the role of business partner. He'd sided with her, convincing Xander to let her be a part of the business.

Stasia pulled her thoughts back to the relevant

subject. "I don't want you going into a deal because you think it'll suit me." When he didn't respond, she raised her voice just enough to gain his attention. "Xander, you aren't listening to me."

"Sure I am. I always listen to you."

She blatantly rolled her eyes. Her brother barely heard a word she said and they both knew it. "Please—"

"Okay. Maybe I get distracted sometimes."

She arched a brow. "Isn't that how you ended up with your new family?"

"Ah, but see how well that worked out." He sent her a smile that lit up his whole face. "I saw a good thing and I went for it."

She couldn't help but tease him. "Is that the story you're going with?"

He shrugged and sent her a guilty smile. "It's how I like to remember it."

Stasia nodded. She didn't mind him rewriting the rocky start of his romance with his now wife, Lea. In fact, Stasia found it endearing. Who knew her brother could be romantic? She never would have guessed it till now.

And as much as she wanted to confide in her big brother about her quandary, she couldn't find the words. She'd been visiting Infinity Island for the past few weeks, reconnecting with her brother and learning more about her sister-in-law, Lea, while playing with the baby, Lily. Stasia had volunteered to babysit while Xander and Lea were working. And though Stasia's days were now full, she still felt as though she was missing something.

As appealing as it was to remain here on this idyllic island with its clear blue water, gentle sea breeze and charming village, she couldn't hijack her brother's life. She'd been here long enough. It was time to head home to Athens.

"Let's go for a walk." Stasia took the last sip of her iced coffee.

Xander scooped up the cruise ticket and then got to his feet. "Lead the way."

She didn't have any particular destination in mind. She just needed to move. "I've never seen you happier."

"I am happy," he said. "My life is complete. And…and I feel guilty."

Stasia stopped walking and faced her brother. "Why should you feel guilty?"

"Because when you were so happy with Lukos, I was being foolish and getting in your way. And by the time I got my head on straight about your husband, he was…well…"

"He was dying." She never thought she'd be able to say those words without breaking into a fit of tears. The memory of losing Lukos far too soon still hurt. She supposed it always would, but she was learning to live with the loss. "It's okay, Xander. You can say he died. I won't break into a million messy pieces."

The look in his eyes said he wasn't sure he believed her. "I miss him too. You do know we got to be good friends at the end."

"I know." The friendship between her husband and brother might not have happened as soon as she would have liked, but she was grateful they'd worked out their differences. She wasn't sure how she'd have made it through that dark period without her brother by her side. "Lukos thought of you like a brother when he died."

Xander reached out and gave her a great big hug. Lukos had made her promise that, no matter what happened in life, she wouldn't let anything come between her and Xander. She'd made the promise. It hadn't been hard. She loved her brother and she always would. She couldn't imagine anything coming between them. He was stuck with his little sister for life.

Xander pulled back and placed the ticket in her hand. "This is your birthday gift. Please take it. I have it on good authority that you always wanted to take the cruise."

She'd only told one person about her desire to cruise around Greece, Montenegro, Croatia and Italy. It would be her trial run to see if she enjoyed voyages before booking something a little farther from home, say the Caribbean, or possibly something a bit cooler, like Norway.

"Lukos told you?" She said it matter-of-factly.

Xander nodded. "He was disappointed he never got to take you on a cruise."

Xander's words took the fight out of her. She'd forgotten all about the things she'd wanted to do before Lukos got sick. They somehow seemed so trivial after all that had happened. Maybe Lukos somehow knew she would feel that way and this was his way of propelling her forward.

And now there were no more excuses—no more reasons to cling so tightly to the past. She needed to fulfill her husband's final wish. She needed to look to the future and find her new path in life.

Her choice needed to be something meaningful. She needed a purpose, a compelling reason to get out of bed in the morning.

Her husband had done his best to watch out for her, leaving her enough money that, when combined with what she'd inherited from her family, it would keep her quite comfortable for the rest of her life. But she couldn't wake up in the morning, enjoy her coffee and drift through the rest of the day. That wasn't how she'd been raised.

She needed a reason to get excited. She needed a goal to strive for and even some setbacks to overcome to remind her of life's many blessings. But what she didn't need was being patted on her head and dismissed because people thought she wasn't up to the challenge.

"Okay. I'll go." She forced a smile to her lips. All the talk of Lukos had deflated her mood. He should be going with her on this adventure, but she knew he would always be in her heart—it just wasn't the same.

"And when you get back, I'll have a business deal or two for you to look over. If one of them isn't to your liking, I'll keep looking until we find the right deal for you."

She didn't say anything about her waning interest in the real-estate market and wanting to strike out on her own. But she wanted a firm plan before she said anything to anyone.

"Thank you." She hugged him again.

This cruise was going to be a turning point in her life. She'd take her laptop with her and make it a working trip. When she got back, she'd have her life all planned out.

DAY ONE

Two weeks later... Athens, Greece

"DID YOU MAKE IT to the ship in time?"

"Why would I be late?" Stasia stood on the busy deck. She pressed the phone to her ear, straining to hear her brother over the voices of dozens of excited travelers.

Xander sighed. "Must you answer a question with a question?"

A smile pulled at Stasia's lips. "Why must you act like the overprotective brother?"

She knew the answer. Xander felt guilty because he was happily married with a baby girl, not to mention living on a private Greek island. And she, well, she was alone now.

Not so long ago, she'd been happy when her college sweetheart had become her husband. Back then, they'd had dreams—lots of dreams. However, it was all cut short when a stomachache turned out to be so much worse than the flu.

From that point, their dreams radically changed. Instead of wishing for exotic vacations, they started wishing for just one more Christmas, one more birthday, one more month, one more day. Stasia halted her thoughts. She pushed away the heart-wrenching memories before she drowned in them.

She'd been on her own for nearly two years now. There had been a lot of tears shed over that time—her first Christmas alone, her first anniversary alone. And when filling out forms, her hand would hover over the *married* box before ultimately checking *single*. It hadn't been easy learning to be a widow—not at all.

Eventually she'd been able to donate Lukos's clothes, including his tailored suits and silk ties. It took a long time until she could bear to slip off her wedding ring and place it with Lukos's in the back of her jewelry box.

Her thumb nervously rubbed over her ring finger. It was something she'd started to do when she'd waited in the doctors' offices and hospital waiting rooms. Feeling the smoothness of her wedding band and knowing the love behind it had somehow bolstered her strength to face the horrible diagnosis Lukos had been given.

She glanced down at her now bare finger.

She was on her own. Each step had taken time. Some steps were big and some were tiny. Each of them had pulled on her heartstrings.

"I… I worry about you." Xander's voice cut through her thoughts.

"I know you do." And she knew it wasn't easy for him to admit it. Xander had always held his feelings close to his chest. "And I appreciate it. But it's okay. I'm okay."

"So you're on the ship?"

She nodded, and then, realizing he couldn't see her, she said, "Yes, I am."

"Good. Now watch out for any smooth-talking men. Don't fall for their lines. Tell them to push off or else your big brother will take care of them—"

"Xander, I'm not in school anymore. I'm a grown woman. I can take care of myself."

Her brother sighed. "I know."

"But you worry."

"Is that a bad thing?"

"No." How could she reprimand him when she'd done something similar when he'd hooked up with Lea? Stasia had posed as a potential buyer of Infinity Island in order to find out if Lea was a gold digger. In the end, Stasia had learned that Lea had a heart of gold. "But you have to trust me. I can take care of myself."

"If you need anything, I'm only a phone call away."

And then a movement out of the corner of her eye caught her attention. It was a tall man with dark hair. Though she could only see the back of him, there was something familiar about the way he held himself and the way he moved with sure, steady strides.

She told herself she shouldn't stare even if it was from across the deck, but she couldn't turn away. Or maybe she was using this distraction to keep from thinking about what her brother was saying. Did Xander really think she was incapable of caring for herself?

She knew then and there that she had to prove to him—to herself—that she could stand firmly on her own two feet. She'd thought she'd been doing that ever since Lukos passed, but it seemed that wasn't so clear to everyone. She promised herself that by the time the cruise ended, she would have a firm life plan for herself.

In the beginning of this horrible nightmare, she'd had her doubts about facing life alone. But one day faded into two, and with each passing day, she'd somehow mustered up the strength and determination to put one foot in front of the other. And now nearly two years later, she was feeling strong and determined. She just needed a direction.

As Xander spoke of the bungalow he could build her on Infinity Island, her gaze focused on that tall, dark man across the way. He was busy speaking with a striking young woman. No doubt it was his girlfriend or wife.

And then the man turned. She was curious to see if his face was as handsome as she'd imagined it to be. And it was, but the surprise didn't end there. The breath caught in her throat.

It was Roberto.

Her heart stuttered. What was he doing here?

Xander had his hand in this. She was certain of it. Her brother couldn't even send her off on a cruise for a birthday gift without feeling the need to send along someone to keep an eye on her.

"What's Roberto doing here?"

"What?"

"Don't act like you don't know what I'm talking about." She was angry. This was too much. "I'm looking right at him."

"I bet he's probably flirting with some beautiful young woman."

"How did you know?"

"Because that's Roberto. He's a *love 'em and leave 'em* kind of guy. If any woman is foolish enough to think he'll commit himself to her, she'll just end up getting hurt. But as far as a friend, they don't come any better than him."

"Xander, I want to know what he's doing on this cruise."

Xander's voice was muffled as though he had his hand over the phone. "Okay. I'm coming." He spoke back into the phone. "Sorry, sis. I've got to go. Lea needs me."

"Xander?"

And with that, the phone went dead.

Stasia inwardly groaned in frustration. What had her brother done? Enough was enough. And she wasn't going to play his game, whatever it was.

This ship was big—big enough for her to avoid Roberto. Which was a shame because she'd always liked Roberto. Even when they were growing up, he'd been kind and thoughtful. And now as an adult, he was the most amazing eye candy.

She hadn't known it was possible for a man to look that good in a suit.

But if he was here to babysit her, then she didn't have time for him. Stasia turned her back to him and walked in the opposite direction. Wherever he was, she would not be.

This was the absolute last place in the world he wanted to be.

Why couldn't a work emergency have come up?

Ding.

Roberto Carrass checked his phone for the ninth time in less than five minutes. The emails were stacking up, each one more important than the last. He didn't have time for a vacation. There was work to be done.

His fingers moved fluidly over the face of his phone. He composed a response to his assistant about a pending acquisition.

Ding. Ding.

Now that he was a full partner with Xander, their business was taking off. There were no more delays, waiting on approvals. When he spotted a good deal, he could move on it—if he wasn't stuck on a two-week cruise with his big Greek family.

Roberto sighed, louder than he'd intended. His phone was not the best way to deal with emails. He really needed to go to his cabin and work on his laptop.

His grandmother elbowed him. "Would you put that contraption away?"

"Yaya, it's a cell phone." With great reluctance, he slipped it in his pocket. "And if you would quit being so stubborn, I would get you one. They aren't that hard to use."

She lifted her chin. "I already have a perfectly good phone at home. I don't need one when I'm out and about. Whatever people want can wait until I get home. Now stop frowning. We're here to have fun." His grandmother smiled brightly. It was so hard to believe she was about to have her eightieth birthday. Most of the time, she acted half her age or younger.

"I'm going to get myself a drink."

Yaya arched a penciled brow. "Don't hide in some corner. Or worse, go to your cabin to work. This is a vacation. Look at all these lovely ladies. I'm sure you'll find someone to spend your time with."

While wearing a forced smile, he inwardly groaned. He was in so much trouble. They'd just pulled out of the dock and they were to be at sea for two weeks—two weeks of matchmaking torture.

"Yaya, I'm fine. I don't need to find someone to spend time with."

His grandmother's gaze narrowed. "Roberto, is there something you haven't told me?"

"Yaya, I—" And then out of the corner of his eye, he thought he saw a young woman he recognized. "I need to go say hello to someone."

The worry lines on his grandmother's face eased. "Don't let me hold you up. I need to go check on your grandfather."

There was something in the tone of his grandmother's voice that caught his attention. "Is he feeling all right?"

His grandmother didn't say anything at first. "I shouldn't say anything."

"It's me. No matter how much he and I argue, I still care. Surely you know that."

"I wish things were different between you two." She sighed. "I don't know what is going on. He won't talk about it. Every time I bring it up, he tells me not to worry."

"But you're still worried?"

She nodded. "Maybe it's nothing."

"Don't worry." He gave her a brief hug. "I'm sure if it's serious, he'll talk to you about it."

"Maybe you could speak to him." Her hopeful gaze implored him.

Roberto gave a quick shake of his head. "I don't think so. It'll just lead to another argument—"

"You don't know that."

"I do. It doesn't matter the subject—eventually it leads back to me abandoning both the company and him. Then an argument ensues."

"Don't you think it's time you two make peace?"

"Tell him. Not me."

She sighed. "I just wish… Oh, never mind. Go mingle."

She didn't have to finish her thought. He knew what she wished—that he was still working with his grandfather. That there was peace in their family.

He leaned over and placed a kiss on his grandmother's cheek. "I'll see you later."

Yaya patted his arm and smiled before she headed off in the opposite direction.

As Roberto walked away, he couldn't stop thinking about his grandparents. They were getting on in years. Was his grandfather doing too much?

This was his grandfather. Obviously he was doing too much. And the look on his grandmother's face said she was more concerned than she let on. With his complicated relationship with his grandfather, he wasn't sure what he could do to help, but for his grandmother's sake, he'd give it some thought.

Roberto didn't waste any time making his way across the deck toward the open-air bar where he'd caught sight of someone who looked quite familiar. Still, the day was quite beautiful with a clear blue sky, warm sunshine and a gentle breeze. Even if he didn't catch up with someone he knew, he might grab a cool drink and find a quiet spot to return a phone call or two before they got too far out to sea and the connection became spotty. He'd been so busy helping Xander spin off a new arm of his real-estate empire, as well as relocating the headquarters to Infinity Island, that he'd forgotten what it was like to have free time. He could once again have a social life.

Roberto intended to stick with his bachelor

status—even if some incorrectly labeled him a playboy. But he couldn't deny his preference for no-strings-attached flings. He didn't have a lot of them, but he wasn't exactly a hermit either.

His bachelor status didn't please his grandparents, who thought he was the age to settle down with a family. All his life there had been expectations set for him. It started back when he was barely out of diapers. He'd been enrolled in the most prestigious preschool. He had to excel at everything so he could attend the top boarding school. And then he was expected to graduate at the top of his class. As the only grandson, his grandparents had high expectations for him.

It was a lot of pressure to put on a kid. By high school, he resented his family's expectations. By college, he was interning at the family construction business. When nothing he did lived up to his grandfather's high standards, Roberto knew he needed to forge a different path—one of his own choosing. And that was what led him to join forces with a childhood friend in the real-estate business, much to his family's disappointment.

Having lost sight of the elusive woman, he moved to the bar and ordered a drink. While he waited, he glanced around once more. Maybe it was just wishful thinking that he'd recognized someone. Still, it had been a good excuse to get away from his grandmother.

He was on his way to an open table off to the side when he spotted her again. This time he was certain he knew her. It was Stasia Marinakos. No other woman carried herself quite like she did, with her slender shoulders pulled back, her head held high and a warm smile on her face. How she could smile after all that she'd been through was beyond him. But she hadn't lost her zest for life. And he applauded her.

"Stasia?" he called out. When she paused and looked around, he called out to her again.

At last, their gazes met. Her big brown eyes widened. He waved her over to join him at the empty table. It took her a moment or two to work her way through the crowd of people all eager to enjoy the morning sun.

"It's so good to see you." He gave her a brief hug.

Was it wrong that he wanted the hug to last a little longer? Of course it was. Stasia was his best friend's younger sister. And if that wasn't enough to discourage any interest, she was a grieving widow. Enough said.

He moved to pull out a chair for her. Once again, her eyes widened with surprise. Was getting her chair for her that unexpected? He mused over this as he returned to his own chair. He supposed that in all of the occasions that they'd spent time together over the years, he hadn't actually spent one-on-one time with her before. There had always been a group of people with them.

She frowned at him. "You don't have to act surprised to see me."

"But I am surprised."

She studied him for a moment. "My brother didn't set this up?" She motioned between them. "Being on the same cruise so you can babysit me?"

"If he did, he didn't mention it to me."

"Oh." She still looked perplexed. "He surprised me with the ticket. He said it was my birthday gift."

"It's your birthday?"

"Not yet. It's next week."

"We'll have to do something special."

"You mean more special than taking an extended cruise?" Her eyes twinkled with amusement.

"Maybe not. But we'll have to mark the occasion." And then he realized she might not be on the ship alone. After all, she'd been a widow for…what was it? Two years. Maybe she was moving on. "Are you sailing alone?"

"I am. How about you? Are you here with someone?"

He wondered if she'd noticed that the passenger list had an overwhelming number of young, beautiful women who appeared to be alone. "I'm not here with anyone. Not exactly."

Stasia arched a brow. "You came on this cruise alone?"

Roberto nodded and surprise flickered in her eyes.

Xander had warned him that he was getting a reputation of always having a beautiful woman on his arm. He'd thought Xander was just having some fun at his expense. Maybe Xander had been serious after all.

"You wouldn't believe that I just wanted to get away from the hustle and bustle of the office?"

She shook her head. "You're just like my brother. You both thrive on the chaotic energy of business. Without it, I think you'd both be bored. In fact, I know it." Her beautiful eyes studied him as though if she stared long enough, layers would peel back, and she'd be able to see what truly made him tick.

Roberto glanced away. Under her gaze, he felt exposed and vulnerable. That was a first for him. He'd sat through a lot of tense meetings with some of the toughest businessmen. They'd all sized each other up for the other's weakness, but none had made him feel like an open book.

He cleared his throat. "Actually, I'm here at my grandmother's request."

The twinkle of surprise showed in Stasia's eyes. "Your grandmother is on the ship?"

He nodded. "So are a number of my family members."

"That must be so nice."

He remained quiet. He knew Stasia only had her brother these days. She didn't know what it was like to have a bunch of well-meaning but intrusive family members delving into her personal life.

"It must be something special to get you out of the office. I hope you have a great time."

And then he realized there wasn't any reason to be secretive. "We're here for my grandmother's eightieth birthday celebration and my cousin's wedding in Venice."

"Wow. That's a lot to celebrate."

He nodded and then glanced around to make sure none of his family were within listening distance. Once he was sure the coast was clear, he leaned closer to Stasia and lowered his voice. "I should probably tell you that my cousin and her fiancé applied to Infinity Island but were turned down."

Stasia's brows rose but she didn't say anything.

"I just wanted to forewarn you because this ship isn't that big, so you're likely to run into them."

"No problem. Thanks for the warning."

He nodded. "I just wonder if it's a good idea for them to get married."

"Why? Don't you like who your cousin is marrying?"

"It's not that." If anything, he really liked Anthony. "He's a great guy. But Xander told me a little of how the system works on Infinity Island. Do you know how the process works?" When she shook her head, he continued. "It seems pretty involved. The legend or folklore or whatever you call it says if you don't pass the test, it means you're ill suited for each other."

"Really? Do you think it's true?"

He shrugged. Weddings were never of interest to him. "I just don't want my cousin to be hurt. She's a great person. Loving and caring."

"I'm sure it'll all work out for her."

This was his turn to study Stasia. It definitely wasn't a hardship. He could stare at her all day. She was beautiful in a very classic and stylish way. Her dark hair was straight and cut in a sleek bob that brushed over the tops of her shoulders. Her makeup only emphasized her vibrant eyes and her high cheekbones. She went for more color when it came to her lips. They were a deep rose shade. Her lips were pouty and inviting.

"Roberto?"

He jerked his gaze back to her eyes. He'd been busted staring. He cleared his throat and glanced away. What had they been discussing?

It took him a second to recall the conversation. "I'm not normally one to give in to such superstitious kind of stuff, but this is my cousin. She's the closest thing I have to a sister."

Stasia reached across the table and squeezed his hand. "I wouldn't worry. There's also this saying that love can overcome everything."

"I sure hope you're right." And then he had a question for her. "If it were you, would you take the test? Would you want to get married on In-finity Island?"

Her eyes didn't give away anything. "That's not a fair question. After all, I'm related to the owners of the island. And as such, I've spent quite a bit of time there. It's a gorgeous place."

"And you still haven't answered my question." It was only then that he realized he was asking a widow about getting married again. He inwardly groaned at his thoughtlessness. "Never mind. I shouldn't have probed. I guess it's just a side ef-fect of my job, always digging for information."

He was about to take a drink when he noticed she didn't have anything in front of her. "Can I get you anything to drink or eat?"

"Actually, yes. I'd love an espresso. I need the caffeine."

It was only then that he noticed the shadows beneath her eyes. They were faint, as though they were covered up, and you wouldn't even notice them unless you were looking for them. Some-thing was keeping her up at night. And then he realized what it might be. She was still grieving for her husband. Sympathy welled up in him.

"I'll be right back with caffeine." He got to his feet and walked away.

He couldn't even imagine what she was going through. It was just one more reason that remaining a bachelor was a good idea. Families were messy with entanglements, emotions and responsibilities. It was easier to just deal with himself.

He ordered two coffees. Though he didn't rely on caffeine to get him up and going in the morning—that was what running was for—that didn't mean he didn't appreciate the flavor and warmth of a cup of coffee.

He'd picked up the coffees and started back to the table when he noticed a young guy headed straight for Stasia. He couldn't blame the guy. She was a beautiful woman. And if she weren't his friend's sister as well as being a widow, he definitely would have pursued her. Nothing serious, but they'd have made some great memories together.

Roberto slowed down, unsure what to do. Maybe Stasia knew the man. Maybe she'd welcome the company. As Stasia smiled at the man, Roberto's body tensed. He knew it shouldn't bother him. It wasn't like the guy was horning in on a date. They'd merely bumped into each other.

Maybe he should head over there and take his

seat. After all, this was his time with Stasia. Was that a thing? Could friends claim time with each other?

Or perhaps he should head to his cabin. He could get some work done before meeting up with his family for dinner. Just then his phone vibrated, letting him know a new email had landed in his inbox.

But instead of withdrawing his phone to find out what required his attention, he continued gazing in Stasia's direction. He wanted to be sure everything was all right before he moved on.

Stasia's smile faded. He couldn't hear what was being said, but the shake of her head let him know she was no longer interested in the man's company. And yet the man didn't move on. Instead the man reached out to touch her. Stasia quickly withdrew her arm.

That was it. The decision had been made for him.

Without giving himself time to reconsider what he was about to do, Roberto headed across the busy deck, weaving and bobbing around the vacationers. He did his best to keep an eye on the situation—it was what Xander would want him to do.

He wondered if Xander had picked this cruise specifically for his sister because he knew Roberto would be on it. If so, it was strange that Xander hadn't mentioned anything to him.

The young man made himself comfortable in his chair and that wouldn't do. Roberto walked up to Stasia. The easiest and fastest way to get rid of her newfound admirer was simple.

"Sorry it took so long, darling." Roberto placed the coffee on the table and then kissed Stasia's cheek.

He noticed the softness of her skin and wondered if her lips would be just as soft. The thought of sneaking in another kiss crossed his mind, but just as quickly he dismissed it.

As Roberto straightened, he noticed the gentle floral scent of her perfume. It was pleasant and fresh like spring. It so suited her because anytime he'd been around Stasia, she'd been sunny and energetic.

The man across the table sat there with his mouth slightly agape as his gaze moved between the two of them. Was it so hard to believe they were together? Sure, he was a few years older than Stasia, but he wasn't an old man by any stretch of imagination.

"I…uh…" The man practically tripped getting to his feet. "Gotta go."

And that was it. The guy turned and made a quick retreat to the bar. Roberto could only wonder if he was seeking a drink to calm his nerves or if he was about to try his luck with one of the young women sitting at the bar.

"What did you do that for?" Stasia's eyes reflected her confusion.

The lack of a smile on her face led him to wonder if he was in trouble. "I saw the guy bothering you." The guy had been bothering her, hadn't he? He hadn't misread her agitation with the young guy, had he? "You weren't interested in him, were you?"

For a moment, Stasia didn't respond. Roberto started to worry he was going to have to track that guy down and apologize. That was about the last thing he wanted to do on this trip.

At last, she shook her head. "I think he was hitting on any available woman on the cruise. I tried to tell him I wasn't interested, but he was the type that didn't take no for an answer." And then her gaze narrowed in on him. "And you couldn't think of any other way to get rid of him other than to act like we're a couple?"

Roberto smiled. "It worked, didn't it?"

She sent him a funny look as though she wasn't sure what to say. Luckily, she didn't know how that innocent kiss had affected him. He'd make sure not to do that again. Getting sucked into Stasia's orbit did strange things to his mind.

Had that just happened?

Stasia resisted the urge to touch her cheek where just moments ago Roberto's lips had been. They'd known each other for years, but they'd never shared a hug, much less a kiss. Usually, it was a passing hello or a nod of recognition.

And it wasn't like he was the first man to kiss her cheek. Why was she letting it get to her like this? When he'd kissed her, her heart had pounded, her mouth had gone dry and her palms had dampened. Sheesh! She really needed to get out more.

She assured herself that it was just the shock of Roberto acting like her significant other. It had caught her completely off guard. Everything would be fine now.

Stasia's mouth suddenly felt dry. She took a large gulp of the strong coffee. That might not have been her brightest idea. She coughed.

Roberto sent her a concerned look. "Are you okay?"

She nodded, then coughed again. "Swallowed the wrong way."

She took a more conservative sip and it calmed her throat. "I should be going. There's so much on the ship to explore. I'm not even sure where to begin."

"They have an app. Did you load it to your phone?" When she looked at him with a blank look, he said, "Could I have your phone?"

She pulled it from a pocket in her black purse and handed it over. He quickly downloaded the app and handed it back to her. "There you go. It'll give you a schedule so you know what's available. Oh, I almost forgot. You should switch your phone to airplane mode to avoid premium roaming charges."

She swiped her finger over the phone until she had the right screen. "Got it."

"And one more thing. You'll want to hook up to the ship's Wi-Fi."

He talked her through the process, and in no time, she was set to go. "Thank you. I wouldn't have thought of that. You must go on a lot of cruises."

"Actually, this is my second. But I do a lot of research. It's one of my hobbies. I research locations, periods in history, all sorts of things. I guess you could say my mind is filled with all sorts of trivia."

"That will come in handy for you."

Lukos had always known how to do those types of things for her. It was just one more thing that she needed to learn to do for herself. The more she did for herself, the more confident she felt.

She smiled at Roberto. "Thank you. I'm sure we'll see each other again."

"I'd like that."

She reluctantly walked away. If given the opportunity, she would have liked to sit and talk the rest of the morning. Roberto had always been easy to be around.

But she had a life plan to brainstorm. Socializing would have to wait for another time. Besides, she couldn't impose on Roberto's time with his family.

DAY TWO

Katakolon, Greece

SO FAR THE TRIP was okay.

Stasia's image came to mind. Maybe the trip was better than okay. Roberto smiled. Much better.

But then there was his grandmother. She was a lady who didn't accept the word *no* from anyone, including him. And right now, she was more interested in his love life than he found comfortable.

Why exactly had he agreed to come on this cruise? Oh, yes, it was his cousin's wedding. And he loved his cousin. But still, wedding bells and his matchmaking grandmother were not a good match. He really should have given this more thought. Perhaps he could have flown in for the ceremony and had the helicopter wait for him after the reception. That would have been much better than enduring the entire trip.

Still, he did have the opportunity to get to know Stasia better. The thought brought another smile to his lips. She was a nice surprise on this ship. At least he had an ally on this voyage.

It was as though his thoughts of Stasia made her appear. She entered the passageway just ahead of him. This trip was definitely looking up.

"Hey, Stasia."

She turned.

He rushed to catch up with her. "Did you make plans for dinner?"

Her forehead scrunched up. "Is this something I should check on my app?"

He chuckled. "I meant to say, do you want to have dinner with me? But if you don't want to or you have other plans, that's fine—"

"No. I mean no, I don't have other plans, and yes, I'd enjoy having dinner with you."

"Roberto! Roberto!"

He didn't have to turn around to know the perky voice belonged to his cousin. If he had a sibling, he'd want them to be just like Gaia. She was so full of life that it bubbled out of her and spread to those around her.

Roberto paused in the passageway. Stasia

stopped next to him and they both turned. His cousin rushed up to him with one of her great big warm smiles. And then she wrapped him in a big hug. He hoped her future husband realized how lucky he was to have Gaia in his life.

When Gaia pulled back, she was still smiling. "We kept missing each other yesterday and I was starting to wonder if you were really on the ship. But I'm glad you're here." It was then that her gaze moved to Stasia. "I'm sorry. I didn't mean to interrupt."

Remembering his manners, he said, "Gaia, I'd like you to meet Stasia Marinakos. Stasia, this is my cousin Gaia, the blushing bride."

"It's so nice to meet you," Stasia said, holding a hand out to Gaia.

"We can do better than that." Gaia hugged a surprised Stasia.

Roberto smiled as Stasia experienced the Gaia effect. When it came to making people feel comfortable and welcomed, his cousin knew how to do it. They may be opposites, but he couldn't love her more if she were his sister.

When the two women parted, Stasia said, "Roberto told me about the wedding in Venice.

Congratulations. I'm sure it will be absolutely beautiful."

Gaia's dark brows drew together. "You sound like you won't be there."

"I… I won't be."

Gaia's puzzled gaze moved from Stasia to him and then back again. "Consider yourself invited. You will be Roberto's plus-one." Gaia's phone buzzed. She glanced at it. "I've got to go. It was so good to meet you." Gaia turned to him and mouthed, "She's great."

Without waiting for anyone to speak, Gaia took off down the passageway.

"What just happened?" Stasia's eyes reflected her confusion.

"That was my cousin. She's kind of like a force of nature."

"But she thinks you and I…that we're a couple. Why didn't you correct her?"

He smiled. "Because she wouldn't care what I said. She likes to come to her own conclusions. She's a lot like our grandmother. She'll figure out the truth eventually."

"And the wedding?"

He paused. His cousin didn't have such a bad idea after all. Weddings made him uncomfortable, especially when his family started asking when he was going to walk down the aisle. His answer was always the same—never.

"What do you think?" he asked. "Would you like to go to the wedding?"

Stasia immediately shook her head. "I couldn't impose."

"You wouldn't be. My cousin is expecting you to be there."

Stasia paused as though considering the idea. "I always did like weddings, and one in Venice has got to be beautiful."

"Good. That's settled." He glanced at his phone and the growing number of emails in his inbox. "I have some work to do, but I'll see you at dinnertime."

They exchanged room numbers and he said he'd pick her up at seven for dinner. Why did that seem so far away? After all, it was already after eleven. After eleven? That meant he didn't have long to work before meeting up with his family for lunch shortly.

This is great. Some downtime to relax and regroup. Maybe Xander had the right idea all along.

Stasia decided not to go ashore at Katakolon. Instead she grabbed her laptop and headed to the deck to enjoy some sun while she did research on her computer. It was time for her to make a plan for the future.

She moved to one of the lounge chairs and sat down. She glanced at her phone and thought about checking out the ship's app. On second thought, she placed her phone in her bag. She didn't have time for fun. She wanted to have a life plan or at least a five-year plan by the time they returned to Athens.

She wondered what Roberto was doing at that moment. Was he having fun with his family? Or was he checking his phone every minute for a new business email? Probably the latter. She smiled. They'd make a good pair on this voyage—each busy with their own endeavors.

The warmth of the sun was so relaxing. Each stiffened muscle loosened. For just a moment, she leaned her head back and closed her eyes.

She hadn't realized until then how much time she'd spent indoors in the past few years. Other than her time on Infinity Island, she'd been inside, at first taking care of Lukos, and then for a number of months after that, she wasn't sure what she did. It was all a blur of tears, regret over all the missed opportunities and then the finality of the paperwork. She never knew there could be so much paperwork involved with a death.

A gentle breeze rushed over her body, cooling it from the sun's rays. If she didn't have so much to do, she could be just like a cat and curl up for a nap in the sun. She really should get to work.

She opened her laptop. Realizing that it was too sunny where she was, she moved to a shaded spot. It was so much easier on her eyes.

She would start with a search engine. She did searches on her interests that included reading and teaching, but she lacked the appropriate degree... Maybe she could go back to school. But the more she thought of it, the more she decided against it.

The afternoon wasn't without its interruptions. It appeared she must have a sign on her forehead that said Single and Alone. Because she was hit on numerous times. Thankfully, the men were charming and respectful when she said she wasn't interested. Still, it was awkward and time-consuming. And the last thing she wanted to do was stay in her cabin for the whole cruise.

She could have stayed home if she were going to do that.

It was almost time for her to get ready for dinner and she still didn't have an idea of how she wanted to focus her life. At the age of twenty-nine, weren't people supposed to have these things figured out? Well, she'd thought she had it all figured out, but then Lukos had been diagnosed with cancer, and it hadn't just affected his life—hers had changed dramatically too.

She shoved the thoughts to the back of her mind. She had a dinner date. Not a *date* date, but dinner with a man who wasn't her brother. The thought spurred her into action. She was actually looking forward to this dinner. Roberto seemed so different outside of the office—much more relaxed and, dare she say it, fun.

At last it was dinnertime.

Roberto couldn't remember the last time he'd been so anxious for a meal. He made his way down the passageway toward Stasia's cabin. His footsteps grew faster.

After a day of touring Katakolon with his family and being introduced to one available woman after the next, he couldn't wait to have the company of an ally. His grandmother had been so upset when he'd almost gleefully told her that he had dinner plans. When his grandmother pushed, he'd admitted that it was Stasia. His grandmother had given him a suspicious look. He hadn't revealed any details, letting her think whatever she wanted so long as she didn't set him up with any other granddaughters of friends.

He had firmly decided that was his last trip ashore with his family. He'd rather stay on the ship the remainder of the cruise than be subjected to his grandparents' tag-team approach to dissecting his life.

The one question he did want to ask his grandmother was how she was able to get all of these single women on this cruise. But he figured he was better off not knowing and pushed the whole matchmaking scenario to the back of his mind.

He double-checked the note he'd made on his phone to remind him of Stasia's cabin number. This was it. He'd just knocked on the door when it was jerked open a crack.

Stasia peered out at him. "You're here?"

He frowned. Had he been so rattled today by his grandmother's blatant matchmaking that he'd mixed up the time in his head? "Weren't we supposed to meet at seven?"

"Oh. Is it that late?" The look on her face was one of panic.

He'd never seen Stasia anything but cool and collected—even at her husband's funeral. Her eyes had told another story, but on the outside, she was elegant and graceful. He'd never known how she'd held it all together so well. If he'd been in her shoes, he'd have been a total wreck, inside and out.

He cleared his throat. "If you need more time, I can come back."

She worried her bottom lip as though considering what to do. And then she shook her head. "You might as well come in."

He wasn't sure what he'd be walking into considering her worried expression. As she swung the door wide open, he took in the sight. On the bed was a pile of dresses that looked like they'd been tried on and then discarded.

"I… I couldn't decide what to wear." Her face bloomed with pinkness that looked totally adorable on her. "I haven't gone to dinner with a man that wasn't my brother since…well, since Lukos."

Roberto nodded in understanding. "It's okay. You can relax. After all, this isn't a date. Right?"

The look on her face was not telling. "Right."

"Do you want help cleaning this up?"

She shook her head. And that was when he noticed she was wearing a strapless black gown with a sequined bodice and a flouncy skirt. She looked... He struggled for a word that did her beauty justice.

"You look amazing." His gaze met hers. The color in her cheeks intensified. "Shall we go?"

"I... I can't. Could you help me?"

"Sure. Whatever you need."

She turned around. "Could you pull up my zipper?"

He told himself not to, but he couldn't resist the temptation of taking in the sight of her bare back. Her smooth skin had a warm bronze tone to it. And in that moment, Stasia had gone from being the sister of his friend to a woman that he desired. He swallowed hard.

He stepped toward her. He told himself that if he did this quickly, it would be all over. The temptation would be gone. And they could return to being nothing more than friends.

Stasia lifted her long hair and swiped it off to

the side, revealing her long, slender neck. It was so tempting to lean forward and plant a kiss on the gentle slope where her neck met her shoulder. He wondered what her reaction would be.

"Roberto? Is there a problem?"

Yes! A great big problem. How am I to remain a perfect gentleman when you look so utterly desirable?

"No. No problem." His voice came out deeper than normal.

Now he had to touch her and act like it was nothing. Otherwise, she would suspect something. And there was no way he wanted to risk their fledgling friendship. He told himself that their friendship was so important to him because she was his only true ally on the ship. Even his cousin was telling him to give romance a chance. Gaia was so happy and she wanted everyone to be just as happy.

He reached out for the zipper. In the process, his fingertips slid across the small of Stasia's back. He noticed the ever-so-slight intake of her breath. So, it wasn't just him who was uncomfortable with this intimate situation.

He grasped the zipper, but it wouldn't budge. How could that be? He pulled harder. Nothing.

Though he didn't want to, he used his other hand to pull the material together, being careful not to touch Stasia's back. He pulled again. Still nothing.

"What's wrong?"

"It's the zipper. It's stuck."

"Stuck?" She attempted to turn around.

"Don't move! You're making it worse."

He pulled gently on the material, clearing it from the teeth of the zipper. He gave it another go. It started to move. He breathed a sigh of relief. His relief was short-lived as the zipper got stuck again.

"This is ridiculous," Stasia said. "I'll just put on something else. Pull down the zipper so I can get out of it."

He tried pulling it the other direction. "It won't budge."

"What?" Concern rang out in her voice. "You mean I'm stuck in this dress that is only half-zipped?"

He needed to get a better view of the zipper. "Move over here."

He walked over and sat on the edge of the bed. This gave him an eye-level view of the problem.

She turned around and took a step toward him.

When her heel caught on the carpeting, she lost her balance. Roberto reached out to her, wrapping his hands around her slender waist. He guided her to him. She landed on his thigh.

She turned to look at him. At this point, her face was mere centimeters from his. The breath caught in his throat as his heart hammered against his ribs. He couldn't ever remember experiencing this powerful of an attraction.

His gaze lowered to her lips. They wore a rosy shade of lip gloss. They reminded him of sun-ripened berries just perfect for picking. But dare he?

When his gaze rose to meet hers, he saw the flames of desire flickering in her eyes. In that moment, she was no one's widow, no one's little sister. She was just a very desirable woman who wanted the same thing as him.

He leaned forward. His mouth lightly brushed hers. He had to move with caution. And then he stopped. Too much, too fast, and she'd bolt. The only sound in the room was the beating of his heart echoing in his ears.

He wanted her so badly, but he wasn't going to rush her. If it killed him, he would sit here and let her walk away. If this kiss were to happen it had to be wanted by both of them.

And then she was there, pressing her lips to his.

At first, her touch was tentative, unsure. He let her lead the way. Right now, he would follow her just about anywhere. Her kiss was sweet and yet it was also spicy. This was a kiss unlike any other—and he'd been kissed a lot. But he knew going forward that Stasia had ruined him for any other woman.

His hand moved to her back. With her zipper stuck, it left her back completely bare. His mouth grew dry. His fingers grazed over the silky-smooth flesh. A moan swelled in the back of his throat. If this didn't stop soon, it would go so much further than either of them was ready for. And he didn't want to lose Stasia—as a friend.

It took every bit of willpower in him to grip her bare shoulders and pull back. Desire and confusion warred within her eyes.

"I'm sorry," he said. "I didn't mean for that to happen."

"Um…you're right." She got to her feet and started to walk away.

"Wait."

She turned back to him. The confusion was still evident in her eyes, but in place of the desire there was now something else. Could it be disappointment? In a blink, whatever he saw was now gone.

He ran his fingers over his mouth. "Your zipper. I need to get it unstuck."

She shook her head. "I'll just change."

"But I don't think you can get out of it until the zipper is fixed."

A distinct frown settled over her beautiful face. He could tell she was considering ways to get out of the dress that didn't involve him touching her again. And it made him feel bad that he'd let go of his common sense and caused this rift between them. He wondered if—no, he hoped—they could move past it.

"Come here." When she didn't move, he said, "The kiss, it won't happen again."

Her eyes reflected the uncertainties churning within her.

"I promise."

That seemed to be enough to get her to move toward him. When Stasia stopped in front of him, he noticed she'd kicked off her high heels. And when she stood with her back to him, she left a modest distance between them. It saddened him that he'd ruined the easiness between them. He would have to work extra hard throughout dinner to gain her trust back.

It took him a few minutes to work the delicate material out of the teeth of the zipper. He slowly pulled on the zipper until it was to the top.

Once she gathered her shoes and purse, he presented his arm to her. For a second, she didn't move. And then she slipped her hand into the crook of his arm. It was a small thing, but it was a start.

What in the world had happened back there?

Stasia's heart still hadn't returned to its normal rhythm. She wasn't sure it would as long as she was with Roberto. She'd always been aware of his devastatingly handsome looks, but she never thought he would be interested in her. She'd seen him in photos on the internet with fashion models, pop stars and countless other beautiful women on his arm, but she never thought she'd be one of them.

The only vision in her mind was of that kiss.

That kiss, it was mind-blowing. It was sinfully delicious. And she hadn't wanted it to end—not ever.

And now that it had, she was struck by a tsunami of guilt. She knew it didn't have to be that way. After all, she'd been a widow for almost two years now. It was past the time for her to move on—at least that was what her friends had been telling her. But it was easier said than done.

Now she was filled with elation that this very sexy man desired her, which was tempered by the thought that she was somehow being unfaithful to her husband's memory. How could she just act like she hadn't pledged her heart and life to Lukos?

Her heart continued to beat wildly in anticipation of feeling Roberto's lips once more. It was traitorous. She was a terrible person.

But then in the back of her mind, she could hear the echo of Lukos's voice. He'd told her she was too young to live the rest of her life alone. He'd insisted she find someone to love and have those kids she wanted. Two of them. A boy and girl.

She'd told him that she would always love him—that their memories would be enough for her. At the time, she'd been unable to imagine her life without Lukos.

He'd pushed and prodded until she'd promised to go on with her life and love again. Tears had been involved on both their parts, but Lukos seemed to relax, knowing she wouldn't give up on life. She wondered what he'd think of her being with Roberto.

Her gaze moved to Roberto. There was absolutely nothing about his stylish haircut, designer suit or flirty smile that said he was ready to settle down. She was worrying too much. It had been a kiss. Nothing more. Everything would be all right.

Once they were seated at their table in the enormous dining room, she ordered a glass of wine. Maybe it would help her relax. She didn't want the evening to be filled with an awkward silence.

"Can we just pretend that it didn't happen?" She hoped he'd agree.

His gaze met hers, and just by looking into his eyes, her pulse raced. What was it about this guy that could make her whole body react to him? It was more than just his great looks. Or maybe she was lonelier than she'd thought.

She needed to focus more on her future and then she'd be less distracted by the Robertos of the world. But right now, there was only one Roberto on her radar. And he didn't seem keen to disregard that steamy kiss.

His voice lowered. It held a sexy rumble to it. "Is that really what you want?"

Her one-word response rushed to the tip of her tongue and teetered there. No. She wanted more of those kisses. Lots more. She would never get enough of them.

But then what? They'd have a steamy onboard affair, and by the time the boat docked back in Athens, she would be left with what? Memories? Would that be enough?

And if she let herself become distracted, she would have no five-year plan for her life. She would be in exactly the same position that she was in now. She couldn't let that happen.

Renewed in her determination to forge her own path in life, she said, "Yes, that's what I would like." But she didn't want to draw a firm line in the sand. "I'd also like it if we could continue our friendship."

There was a flicker of something—could it be

disappointment in his eyes? Or was she just seeing what she wanted to see?

"I would like that very much." He sent her a warm, reassuring smile. "Now wait until I tell you about my day."

It didn't take long for the awkwardness to fade away. They ordered their dinner and relaxed. Roberto's day had been anything but boring. And Stasia felt bad for him, not only being set up on a lunch date, but also two other dates that afternoon. And if it hadn't been for their dinner plans, he would be having dinner with some other young woman.

Stasia sipped her wine. "And here I thought my brother was bad with his overprotective tendencies."

"Xander just wants what is best for you."

"Don't start sticking up for him or I might have to rethink this whole arrangement." And then she sent him a teasing smile.

Roberto held up his hands in surrender. "I have no interest in getting between two siblings."

"Smart man. I knew there was a reason I liked you."

They both smiled and the rest of dinner was filled with light conversation as well as laughter.

By the end, Stasia had to admit that she hadn't had this much fun in…well, in a very long time. And she hated to see it end. But she knew she couldn't occupy all his time.

"Would you like dessert?" Roberto offered.

She shook her head. "I'm full. The meal was delicious. I must admit that I had my doubts about onboard dining, but they have most definitely put my worries to rest."

Roberto set aside his napkin. "Thank you for joining me. This dinner was definitely the best part of my day." His smile faltered and she had to wonder if he was recalling their kiss. "Would you like to do anything else?"

She best not press her luck. "Thank you for the offer, but I should be going."

"Maybe we can share a meal again while we're sailing."

"I'd like that." She would like that a whole lot—so much so that it scared her.

And with that, they parted company. She went one way and he went the other. She should head back to her cabin to start reading some of the self-help books she'd purchased. Some people would think that she was silly or perhaps frivolous for not having a clear path in life. But when your future was stolen away by cancer you had to regroup. That was what she was doing.

But she found that she was too wound up to concentrate on reading just yet. She told herself it was the lively dinner conversation and that it had absolutely nothing to do with that earth-moving kiss back in her cabin. Either way, she decided a walk around the deck might be nice.

She found that she wasn't the only one wanting to enjoy the warm evening under the stars. But most of the people around her were coupled up. Some were arm in arm; others were stealing a kiss in the moonlight.

Stasia, in that moment, felt profoundly alone. There was no one waiting back in her cabin for her. Her thoughts turned to Roberto, but she halted them. She would be fine alone.

"There you are."

Roberto paused in the hallway. "Hello, Yaya."

"Did you have a good dinner?"

"I did. Thank you. And how was yours?"

She gave a nonchalant shrug of her shoulder. "It was nothing special. Marissa was sorry you couldn't have joined us."

Marissa must be another attempt at matchmaking. "Like I said, I had a prior commitment. And I didn't want to cancel at the last moment." He knew how his grandmother felt about manners—even when it foiled one of her matchmaking schemes.

"Perhaps tomorrow when we dock, you could make it up to Marissa." His grandmother's eyes twinkled with renewed hope.

"I have plans." He was going to ask Stasia to go sightseeing with him. The idea had just come to him, but he liked the idea of spending the day with her. He liked it quite a lot. "I'm sorry, Yaya. I must go. I have to meet someone."

His grandmother's eyes narrowed. "Is this someone a female?" When he nodded, she asked, "The same one you dined with?" When he nodded again, she asked, "And you still maintain that you're nothing more than friends?"

The answer to that question was more complicated than the last time she'd asked it. He drew in a deep breath as he considered his options. He never lied to his grandmother. He might not always give her full and complete answers, but never an outright lie.

He continued to meet her inquisitive stare. "It's complicated."

His grandmother's eyes widened. "You have feelings for this girl?"

Ding.

He'd never been so happy to receive an email.

"I have to go. I have some business that needs my immediate attention." The truth was that he didn't know how he felt. That kiss, it had affected him more than he'd expected.

He headed for the deck to get some fresh air before he spoke with Stasia. He didn't want to do anything foolish. The more time he spent with Stasia, the more he liked spending time with her. And therein lay the rub. He stepped out on the spacious deck, and as though his thoughts had summoned her, there stood Stasia, staring out at the vast sea. Like a magnet, he was drawn to her.

He stepped up behind her. "We meet again."

Stasia turned to him and smiled, making his chest get that funny, warm sensation again. "I was just going to take a walk. Would you like to join me?"

"I can't think of anything I'd like more." Because it was the gentlemanly thing to do, he offered her his arm.

And this time, without hesitation, she accepted. When she slipped her hand into the crook of his arm, he could feel the warmth of her touch through the fabric of his dinner jacket. He liked that feeling—very much so.

They set off, strolling along the moon-drenched deck, looking like every other star-crossed lover enjoying their evening with the one they loved. Except they weren't in love, he reminded himself. Sure, they'd kissed, but that had been a mistake. The best mistake he'd ever made.

As the other couples headed inside, they strolled for a while in the quiet of the evening. The only sounds around them were of the sea and occasionally when a door was opened, voices from within trickling out to them.

"You know, we're docking in Corfu tomorrow. Would you like to go with me on the guided tour and check out some ancient ruins?"

Stasia shook her head. "Thank you. But I don't think so."

"What? You don't like history?"

"It's not that. It's just that I have some stuff I need to do."

She made it sound like work. And he couldn't imagine what work she would have to do while on vacation. Xander had sent his sister on this trip for her to relax and unwind. Her sitting in her cabin working while he was out sightseeing didn't seem right.

"Come with me for just a little while."

She turned a questioning glance his way. "You really want me to go sightseeing with you?"

He nodded. "It'd be nice to see it with a friend."

She hesitated. He implored her with his eyes. He didn't know why this was so important to him, but it was.

"All right. I think an outing would be nice." Stasia smiled at him, making his heart pound harder than normal.

"It's a date." Once the words had left his lips, he knew it was a mistake. But when she didn't correct him, he let it go.

He escorted Stasia back to her cabin, and it seemed so natural to lean in and give her a kiss good-night, but he caught himself just in time. After they agreed on where to meet in the morning, they said good-night. Stasia slipped inside the cabin and a feeling of disappointment fell over him by missing out on that kiss.

DAY THREE

Corfu, Greece

THERE HAD BEEN so much to see.

And they'd hardly covered much of the Mediterranean island, even though they'd set off first thing in the morning. It was now late in the day.

They'd joined a guided tour that took them to one of the island's picturesque beaches. They didn't tarry long as they moved on to the Royal Palace, also known as the Museum of Asian Art, with its stunning collection of artifacts from China, Japan and India.

From there they'd visited Corfu's old town, with its narrow roads and older homes. It was like an archaeological treasure trove.

And Stasia's feet were sore from all of the walking. "That was beautiful."

"Yes, you are." Roberto smiled at her.

Stasia couldn't help but laugh at his very obvious flirting. He had been the perfect date today.

He'd been fun, distracting, and most of all, he hadn't treated her like she was fragile, like her brother and friends did. While touring Corfu, she hadn't thought about all the things that had been weighing on her mind. The museum was interesting and the artifacts were definitely worth a closer look.

But now with evening approaching, they boarded the ship with the other tourists. Stasia was exhausted from all the walking, but she didn't regret a moment of it. Who knew Roberto had such a relaxed side to him? In his short sleeves and khaki shorts, he looked like a laid-back tourist. At this particular moment, he was the exact opposite of the serious businessman who she'd gotten to know over the years.

Once on the deck, Stasia moved off to the side and turned to Roberto. "Thank you for today."

He was still smiling. "So you're not mad that I practically twisted your arm to go?"

"Not at all." And just so he knew she meant it, she lifted up on her tiptoes to give him a hug.

At first, he didn't move. And she wondered if she'd overstepped in their friendship. But then his arms wrapped around her, pulling her close. She breathed in his masculine scent mixed with a light whiff of spicy cologne. She longed to lean in closer to inhale the intoxicating combination—

"Hello, Roberto."

The woman's voice had Stasia jerking back out of his embrace. Heat swirled in her chest and raced to her cheeks as she turned to face the person. The older woman's silver hair was trimmed short and not a strand was out of place. Diamond earrings adorned her ears. And her face was made up. But it was her gray-blue eyes that caught and held Stasia's attention. They were the exact same shade as Roberto's. She didn't have to be told. This was his grandmother.

"Yaya, what are you doing here?" Roberto asked.

"Why, dear, this is a ship. And I was out for a stroll." Her gaze moved between him and Stasia. "Maybe I should be asking the questions. What is going on here? You have a dinner date with Marissa."

"We already ate while we were ashore," Roberto said.

His grandmother's eyes darkened. "You knew you had obligations."

Stasia couldn't believe his grandmother was

really going to push her agenda, even in front of her. Stasia's heart went out to Roberto. At least Xander wasn't pushing her into some man's arms to get her out of his hair. In fact, Xander would probably do the opposite and keep her away from any men.

But she just couldn't stand there and let Roberto's grandmother push him to do things he didn't want to do. And he loved his grandmother too much to stand up to her and cause a rift. So that left Stasia. She could fix this problem. But did she dare?

Catching sight of a beautiful woman headed in their direction with her gaze set on Roberto, Stasia slipped her hand in his. Roberto turned a surprised look at Stasia.

"You might as well go ahead and tell your grandmother," Stasia said.

"Tell me what?" His grandmother's gaze moved between the two of them.

Roberto's eyes reflected his confusion. He stared deep into Stasia's eyes, searching for answers. She hadn't thought this was going to be so stunning for him. Perhaps she needed to help him a bit.

"Go ahead and tell her about us." Was it her

imagination or had his complexion lost a bit of its color?

He shook his head. "I don't think this is a good idea."

"Roberto, tell me what is going on," his grandmother demanded.

Roberto was still staring into Stasia's eyes. "You're sure about this?"

She sent him a reassuring smile and nodded.

He turned to his grandmother. "Stasia and I are involved."

"You are a couple?" His grandmother's gaze narrowed. When they both reluctantly nodded, his grandmother asked, "Then why did you tell me that you weren't involved when I asked before?"

Stasia tightened her grip on his hand, sensing the tension coursing through his grandmother's inquisition. Stasia had never done anything like this before, but she'd never met anyone quite so pushy. What was Roberto going to tell the woman?

Roberto cleared his throat. "Stasia is my friend's sister. I don't think Xander will be happy to know we're involved. In fact, I'm quite certain he'll be anything but happy. So, you see, it's for the best that we keep this quiet."

The beautiful young woman stepped up next to Roberto's grandmother. "Is it time?"

"Not now, dear." Roberto's grandmother never took her gaze off Stasia and Roberto long enough to look at the young woman. "I'll catch up with you later."

The young woman frowned. "But I thought—"

"I'll explain later. Now go." His grandmother's voice brooked no room for argument.

With a dark look at Stasia, the young woman turned on her stilettos and strode away. It was then that Stasia wondered if she'd helped or hindered Roberto. After all, that young lady was amazingly beautiful.

The older woman's eyes held a glint of skepticism. She narrowed her view in on Stasia. "Is this true? Are you seeing my grandson?"

"Yes."

"Hmpf…" The woman's gaze moved from her to Roberto. "We'll talk more about this later." And with that, his grandmother strode away.

When the woman was out of earshot, Stasia asked, "Do you think she believed me?"

"I don't know. It's tough to get anything past her."

"I feel bad about deceiving her."

"So do I, but it wouldn't be necessary if she'd give up on trying to find me a wife." His gaze met hers. "She isn't the only one to worry about. If your brother finds out, he truly isn't going to be happy."

"You're right. If he ever found out, he would be furious with both of us. He can be so protective. Did you know that when I got married we had to elope because Xander didn't approve of Lukos?"

Now, why had she gone and dredged up that memory? Perhaps because Lukos was such a big part of her life and pretending otherwise was impossible.

Their wedding had been simple but romantic in a small rustic chapel in the rolling hills of Tuscany. She'd worn a simple white dress while holding a bouquet of wildflowers. Lukos had worn a dark suit and tie while wearing a huge smile that lit up the whole world. Stasia stifled a resigned sigh.

She should have known then that something was wrong with him. But she explained away his symptoms as being stress over fighting with her brother and then the wedding. How was she supposed to have known—known that he was dying? Still, she should have suspected that it was something more.

Stasia drew in an unsteady breath as she slammed the door on her memories. And the pain, she tucked away deep inside her heart.

Roberto studied her with a frown on his face. "I'm sorry. I didn't mean to upset you."

"I… I'm fine." She said the words, trying to convince herself as much as him. "It's just sometimes I wish I could go back and do things differently."

"I knew back then there was some trouble between you and Xander. I just didn't know the details."

"Xander later apologized, saying he'd misjudged Lukos. But in the beginning, you could slice the tension in the room with a knife." She shook her head, chasing away the unhappy memories. "I know Xander loves me and only wants the best for me, but I wish he'd trust me to figure that out on my own. My whole life, it's felt like he's been smothering me with his overprotectiveness. He'd scare off the guys when I was in school. I used to have to sneak around to date."

"As I recall, you did some butting into his romance with Lea."

Roberto was right, but she'd had her reasons. "That was different. He didn't even know her all that long and all of a sudden he's moving to Infinity Island."

"He didn't move there in the beginning—"

"It sure seemed like it. How was I to know if Lea was telling the truth about being pregnant? And it being his child?"

"But it wasn't up to you to know the truth. That was his situation to settle for himself."

Stasia frowned. Roberto was right. She had done exactly what she'd accused her brother of doing—butting in. "So, what do we do about Xander?"

"We don't tell him about our little shipboard arrangement."

"I don't want to lie to him."

"You won't be. It's not like we're actually involved. What my grandmother makes up in her own mind is all up to her."

Stasia's mind was still stuck on them pretending to be romantically involved and what all that would entail. "We'll be a couple for the voyage and then what?"

"We break up. It isn't that far-fetched. Couples do it all of the time."

"But why would we break up?" She was having a hard time imagining why any woman would walk away from Roberto.

"I work too much. I'm too much of a neat freak. I'm no fun."

"As for the first one, that could be changed with enough encouragement." She smiled at him.

He smiled back. "Perhaps with the right person."

As he continued to look directly at her, her heart raced. Surely he didn't mean she was the right person. Of course not. Right?

She averted her gaze. It was the only way she could string words together. "As for the second reason, I admire a man who cleans up after himself."

"Oh, so that's a positive quality."

"Very much so." She was having fun with the flirty banter. It'd been so long since she'd felt like a desirable woman and not like a nursemaid or a fragile widow. "As for the last reason, well, that is obviously not true. I had a lot of fun today. And I'm looking forward to more excursions."

"I must admit that when I first suggested the tour of Corfu, I wasn't so sure about it. You're the one who made it fun."

"I think we made it entertaining together. So when do we arrive in Venice?"

"Not for a few days."

And then she came to a stop outside her cabin. "Can you believe I've never been to Venice?"

"Really? I would have thought you'd have visited the beautiful city at least once."

"I've always meant to. But for one reason or another, I've never been there."

He smiled at her. "I'm honored that your first visit will be with me."

She gazed into his eyes and her heart skipped a beat. Again, she was swept up in the desire to lift up on her tiptoes, press her hands to his broad shoulders and touch her lips to his. Stasia stifled a sigh.

At the very least, it would be nice to invite him into her cabin for a nightcap. She knew what would happen if she did. This pretend relationship would take on a very real tone. And she knew that would not only jeopardize Roberto's relationship with Xander, but it would also gravely injure her brother-sister relationship. That was a lot to risk for a shipboard romance that would end as soon as they returned to Athens.

Left with no reasonable option to prolong their time together, her gaze lifted to his. "Good night."

"Night."

She remained right there in her doorway as he turned and walked away. Her gaze lingered on him. He looked just as fine going as he did coming. Mighty fine indeed.

DAY FOUR

Kotor, Montenegro

KEEPING UP APPEARANCES surprisingly wasn't hard.

Roberto liked spending time with Stasia. In fact, it was quite possible he liked it too much. But Stasia wasn't quite as enthusiastic. Granted, his boisterous family could be a lot to take in all at once. But every chance Stasia got, she would escape to her cabin. Or perhaps it just felt that way to him because he missed her when she wasn't around.

"You're a hard man to catch up with," said a familiar male voice.

Roberto turned to find his grandfather standing behind him. "I don't mean to be. There are just a lot of activities on this ship and then there are the daily tours and there's also work to catch up on. I'm always on the go."

"I understand. Your grandmother has tried

to get me to go on the tours with her, but she doesn't understand that I have work to do."

Roberto felt bad for his grandfather. He wasn't getting any younger, and at his age, he should be able to enjoy life instead of having to worry about work and deadlines. But there was this thing about control. His grandfather didn't want to give it up. His successor would have to meet his stringent requirements. As of now, no one in the family wanted the position or was willing to meet his grandfather's standards—including himself.

His goal since childhood was taking over his grandfather's commercial construction business. But in college, when he'd gotten into it with his grandfather over the man's unreasonable expectations, Roberto had walked away. He'd joined Xander and he'd helped his friend build up his real-estate company.

His grandfather cleared his throat, drawing Roberto from his thoughts. "I have to be going."

"To meet Yaya?"

His grandfather shook his head. "I told her I didn't have time for a cruise right now."

He knew his grandfather was a workaholic, but

this seemed excessive even for him. "Is something wrong?"

His grandfather frowned. "Don't start sounding like your grandmother. She's always on me about slowing down."

When Roberto was younger, he would have let the subject drop, but now that he was older, his grandfather was still stubborn and quite set in his ways but not nearly as intimidating. "Maybe she has a point."

His grandfather's mouth pressed in a firm line as he glared at Roberto as though he were some sort of traitor. When Roberto refused to back down, his grandfather sighed.

"It's not like you care. You left."

"I left the company because you didn't give me a choice." Before his grandfather could vocalize his protest, Roberto continued. "But let's leave it in the past."

"You had a choice." His grandfather liked to have the last word. Roberto braced himself for an argument, but then his grandfather said, "I suppose there's no point in rehashing it."

For a moment, Roberto wasn't sure he'd heard his grandfather correctly. Considering his grandfather's congenial mood, Roberto decided to extend an olive branch. He knew it was risky because his grandfather's responses were so unpredictable. But then he thought of his grandmother and knew he had to try to help.

"You know, I have some time during the cruise and I'm not much of a sightseer. If you have some work to throw my way, it'd give me an excuse to get out of some of the planned excursions."

His grandfather frowned. "If this is some sort of charity—"

"It's not." Roberto shook his head in frustration. He should have known his grandfather wouldn't change. "Never mind—"

"Wait." His grandfather stared at him as though trying to decide if this was the right decision. "If you're serious, I could use another set of eyes. But this has to remain confidential. I don't want your grandmother to worry."

It was a little late for that, but Roberto decided to play along. It must be bad if his grandfather was willing to give in that easily.

This was the first time his grandfather had ever asked for his input. "Sure."

His grandfather gave him a brief idea of the large project taking place on the outskirts of Athens. And then using his smartphone, his grandfather forwarded Roberto the pertinent files. The fact that his grandfather used a smartphone impressed him. Not everyone his grandfather's age kept up with technology. But then again, not everyone his grandfather's age was still running a multimillion-dollar corporation. Roberto promised to get back to his grandfather by the end of the cruise.

"Now that we have that out of the way, tell me how serious this relationship is with…what's her name?" his grandfather asked.

"Stasia. Did Yaya tell you that we're involved?"

His grandfather was a tall man with a full head of gray hair. The lines of time that marked his face only made him look more distinguished and wiser. He arched a brow as he stared at his only grandson. "Wasn't she supposed to tell me? Seems like the rest of the family is getting to know her."

Roberto resisted the urge to shrug his shoulders. It was one of those gestures that got on his grandfather's nerves. He thought that it was lazy and ill-mannered. When Roberto was a child, his grandfather would always correct him and insist Roberto use his words.

Roberto cleared his throat. "I'm just surprised

is all. The relationship is new. And Yaya didn't appear pleased about it."

"She doesn't think you're serious about this woman. She thinks you're avoiding the opportunity to meet some nice young ladies." His grandfather's pointed stare met his. "Is she right?"

"Why does it have to be serious?"

His grandfather narrowed his gaze on him. "What you're saying is that this isn't going to be anything permanent either. I have to wonder if you're even involved with Stasia."

Heated words rushed to the back of Roberto's throat. Why did his grandfather always look at him like he was a failure because he refused to do things the way his family thought they should be done? At least he was still here, unlike his parents, who were married but lived separate lives in separate parts of the world—separate from him.

Roberto wasn't going to do what his grandfather wanted just to fit in and not make waves. His parents had done that, and now they were unhappier than any two people he knew. As it was, his grandparents had raised him because his parents couldn't stand being at home for any length of time.

His early childhood had been a series of nannies. His parents had worked in the family business and socialized regularly. They were either too busy or too exhausted to deal with him.

At one point, Roberto recalled overhearing his mother saying that she regretted having him. Those words had been seared upon his heart. He withdrew from people. Even at the age of seven, he knew not to trust people because in the end they'd hurt you.

And then a huge fight between his father and grandfather had his parents packing and leaving—without him. Much later, Roberto learned there had been accusations against his parents of mismanagement and harassment.

Roberto spent the remainder of his youth moving between his grandparents' vast estate and boarding school. His grandmother tried her best to fill the void in his life, but being abandoned by his parents left a scar that couldn't be erased, no matter how hard his grandmother tried.

Roberto had vowed long ago not to have a family. He didn't want to find out after the fact that he wasn't cut out to be a father—just like his parents. He refused to subject a child of his own to a life like that.

But what about Stasia? Did she want a family? Sure, she'd made moves to join Xander in the business world, but something told him her heart wasn't in it. He'd noticed her sometimes at the meetings with Xander. She'd been attentive and interacted, but she hadn't smiled. Her face hadn't been animated like it was when she got truly excited about something.

However, she had seemed happy when she was married. Was that what she wanted again? If it was, he'd have to be careful. If things between them escalated, he didn't want to get her hopes up that he could offer her a diamond ring. It would never happen.

His gaze met his grandfather's. "You don't have to wonder. Stasia and I are together. She'll be attending the wedding with me."

"We'll see how long this lasts." And then his grandfather strode away.

Roberto shrugged off his grandfather's disappointment. It was something he'd grown accustomed to over the years. Some things didn't change.

His thoughts turned to Stasia. He wondered what she was doing right now. He thought of seeking her out, but then changed his mind. It was best not to spend too much time together—even if a part of him wanted to spend all his time with her.

It was too beautiful to stay in the cabin.

Stasia lifted her face to the warm sunshine. Maybe she should have taken Roberto up on his offer to take her on today's tour. Where had they stopped? It took her a second to figure out which port they were at that day. With them sailing at night and docking at a new port each morning, it was a lot to remember. But then she recalled that today they were in Montenegro. Though exploring the old Mediterranean town appealed to her, she was holding out for Venice. She couldn't wait to explore as much of it as time allowed.

In the meantime, she'd spent the morning in her cabin poring over aptitude tests and college catalogs and then running internet searches. She stared at her computer until her head started to pound.

She wondered what Roberto was doing, but she didn't want to disturb him, as she didn't want to take up all his time. It wouldn't be fair. He deserved to spend his vacation any way he pleased—even if it meant working.

She'd made her way to the pool. There were a lot of young families around. The echo of children's voices surrounded her. As she found an available lounge chair, she couldn't help thinking she'd been robbed of this experience with Lukos. They'd been planning on having a baby. In fact, they'd just started working on a family when he'd received the most devastating news that he had cancer. For a man who'd exercised regularly and led a healthy lifestyle, this diagnosis came as quite a shock to both of them.

A little boy moved past her chair, holding on to his father's hand. The little boy must be around two…about the age her child would be if their attempt at starting a family had been successful. An arrow of pain shot through her heart.

While Lukos had been in the hospital, he got to the point where he would send her away. Lukos liked to read or as he grew sicker he'd listen to audiobooks during his treatment. She never wanted to go far from him and so she'd made her way around the hospital. She'd ended up learning about all the volunteer programs out there. They'd intrigued her as she'd visited with the children as well as the elderly.

"Stasia?" Roberto's voice drew her attention.

She turned to the side, finding him heading for her. He was wearing shorts that showed off his long, lean runner legs. Her gaze rose up over his trim waist, broad chest and strong arms. When she reached his clean-shaven chiseled jaw, she paused. Her gaze lingered over his very kissable lips. With a bit of a struggle, she drew her attention upward past his straight nose and stopped at his gray-blue eyes. There was amusement reflected in them.

She swallowed hard. She didn't normally get caught checking someone out. In fact, she wasn't in the habit of checking anyone out. But there was something about Roberto—something that had her thinking about what it'd be like to start over.

"Find something you liked?" he asked in a teasing tone.

Heat rushed to her face. "I… I just didn't expect to see you today."

"I can leave if you want—"

"No, please stay."

He took a seat next to her. "I took care of some emails this morning, but I didn't have anything else planned for the day."

"So you aren't a businessman twenty-four-seven?"

His brows lifted. "Is that what you think?"

She shrugged. "It kind of seems that way."

He didn't say anything for a moment as though mulling over her words for some validity. "I guess you've only seen me at the office and at business events. But I do other things."

"Such as?" She was genuinely curious to know the other side of this man.

"I like to go running early in the morning just as the sun is rising."

"It shows in those shorts. You have very nice legs." Was that a bit of color in his cheeks?

"And I like to cook, but I must admit I don't bother very often. More times than not I eat take-out at my desk. I always tell myself I'm going to leave the office at a reasonable hour but then I get engrossed in a project and lose track of time."

"Or is it that you don't have a reason to go home?" That was what happened when she visited Infinity Island. It was so hard for her to leave her adorable niece and family in order to return to a house full of nothing but memories.

It was funny how life played out. In the beginning, she was the one who found love at an early age, and for a long time, she worried Xander would never know such happiness. And now Xander was the one with the love of a family and she was the one walking through life alone. Life could be so unpredictable.

Roberto averted his gaze. "I've chosen work over a home life. It's the way I like things."

She wanted to argue, but she couldn't. Choosing a career over having a family sounded much safer. "Maybe you're right."

This time his gaze did meet hers. Questions reflected in his eyes. "I'm right?"

She struggled not to laugh at his shocked expression. "Why do you look so surprised?"

"Because, well, no one has ever agreed with me before."

There was a time when she wouldn't have agreed with him either. But that boat had sailed, so to speak. Maybe it was time to let him in on her special project. "I've been looking for a job—but not just any job. I want one that fulfills me the way work does you and my brother."

"I thought you were going to join Xander in some real-estate deals."

She glanced away, catching sight of a little boy and his father rolling a bright red ball back and forth. "Don't tell Xander, but real estate, it's not for me."

"Really? Because you seemed so anxious to work on the resort in Italy."

"You're right. I was, in the beginning. But I was mostly excited about being able to work side by side with my brother."

"So what happened?"

It'd been a long time since someone was truly interested in her and her feelings. "I don't know. Somewhere along the way, I figured out that this deal was really involved and long lasting. I just couldn't imagine having my life tied to the project for years. It was just too cold—too impersonal." She caught the frown flitting across Roberto's face and realized how her words might hurt him. "I'm sorry. I didn't mean you and my brother can't find happiness in the work. It's just not for me."

"Fair enough. So what do you want to do?"

"That's the problem. I don't know. I know how ridiculous that sounds for an almost twenty-nine-year-old to not know what they want to do with their life. I married young, and with Lukos's job, I knew we would be traveling a lot. I was all right with putting aside my career to support him, and we were talking—well, we were doing more than talking—about having a family. And then, well, you know...he got sick." She sucked in a steadying breath. "So now I have no husband, no baby and no idea what to do with the rest of my life."

Roberto reached out and took her hand in his. He gave it a squeeze. "I'm sorry. Life isn't fair."

"Agreed." But they'd been talking about her for far too long. "So how about you?"

"What about me?"

"I don't know, but we've discussed my life enough for one day. Tell me something new about you."

"Well, I just spoke with my grandfather. He needs my help."

She wasn't sure what to say at this point. His furrowed brow told her that whatever his grandfather had asked of him must be weighing on him. She wasn't sure if it was her place to press him for information.

Roberto turned to her. "You have to understand that my grandfather has never asked for my help. My grandparents stepped up and raised me when my dysfunctional parents abandoned me. I don't know what I'd have done without them. But I'm afraid I've failed them. I haven't followed the path they wanted for me—working in the family business."

"I always wondered about that. But I knew you had your reasons."

Roberto got quiet. He stared off into space as though he were thinking something over. By the creased lines on his forehead, it was troubling him.

"It must be serious."

Roberto shrugged. "I'm not sure. He said he had some reports for me to look over, but he was reluctant to go into details."

"That's rather mysterious, isn't it?"

"Yes, very. My grandfather isn't one to play games. He's a straight shooter. But I'm sure you don't want to hear about my family business."

"I'm interested in whatever you want to share with me. And it's nice to focus on someone else's problems for once. I'd like to think that we're friends besides being fake lovers."

"We're definitely friends."

"Good. I was hoping you'd be up for touring Venice with me. We'll arrive there in a couple of days." It was heralded as one of the most romantic cities in the world and it just seemed like a place that she would like to share with some-one—even her fake boyfriend.

He reached out and gave her hand a squeeze. "You can count on it."

His touch warmed her skin and sent a shiver of excitement over her. What was it about this man that got her body all excited with just a touch?

Her gaze met his and held. She knew she should turn away, but she lacked the willpower. There was something mesmerizing about his eyes, as though they could see straight through her and read her very thoughts.

She wondered if he could sense that all she wanted to do on this beautiful day was get lost in his arms and revisit the kiss he'd laid on her the other day. If only someone would come flirt with her, perhaps Roberto would kiss her again.

All too soon, Roberto released her hand and got to his feet. "I've taken up enough of your day. I'll let you get back to your planning."

As he turned to walk away, she wanted to call out to him to stay. She wanted to tell him that she could figure out her future another time. But wasn't that what got her in this tough spot in the first place? And without a definite plan by the time the cruise ended, she would end up caving to Xander's plans because she wouldn't want to hurt him.

And there was another reason she needed to hold back. This rush of emotions felt so new— so foreign. How could she possibly be falling for Roberto? Or was she just trying to fill that void in her heart?

Either way, she needed to slow things down. She didn't trust herself where Roberto was concerned. And so she remained quiet as he moved out of sight.

DAY FIVE

Dubrovnik, Croatia

VENICE SEEMED SO far away.

Luckily Roberto hadn't meant to keep his distance until then.

Stasia sat across the table from him. They'd just had lunch. Neither felt like going ashore. Instead they'd moved to the deck beneath the light blue sky. To keep up appearances with his family, they were spending a lot of time together. Every day they gravitated toward each other, and to Stasia's surprise, she didn't mind. In fact, she was enjoying having a friend on board.

While Roberto enjoyed an iced latte that she'd convinced him to try, she was sipping on a fruity umbrella drink. A gentle breeze rushed over her sun-warmed skin as they sat in comfortable silence.

"Roberto?" a female voice called.

In the next moment, his grandmother and a

gentleman with silver hair who resembled Roberto, from his handsome face to his tall stature, approached. The man had some white in the temples that only accentuated his classic good looks. It was definitely Roberto's grandfather. However, neither grandparent was smiling.

Roberto rose to his feet and gave his grandmother a hug. "Yaya, happy birthday."

"Thank you," his grandmother said. "Everything is arranged for the party this evening." And then his grandmother smiled. Not one of those friendly, doting grandmotherly smiles, but one of those I-know-something-you-don't-know smiles. And even though Stasia didn't know the woman, it made her nervous.

"Good." The straight line of Roberto's shoulders eased. "Is there anything you need me to do—"

"Yes." His grandfather spoke up. "I thought you'd be in your cabin working on that project I gave you." The man frowned. Displeasure was written all over his face. "I should have known better—"

"I was just headed that way to get my laptop."

His grandfather's eyes widened in surprise. "I'm looking forward to hearing your thoughts."

"And you don't want to give me a heads-up about what I'll be looking for?"

He shook his head. "I want your unbiased opinion about the numbers."

"Okay. I'll do my best."

"You have until the end of the cruise."

Stasia felt for Roberto. How was he supposed to do what his grandfather wanted when the man was being so vague? And by the look on Roberto's face, no matter what he said, pleasing his grandparents was important to him. He may have fooled himself into thinking otherwise, but she could see the love he had for them written all over his face. And she couldn't blame him.

Family was something special—something she no longer had. And now that Xander was married with a child of his own, he felt further away than ever before. And that was why she needed to carve out a life for herself. She needed to find a job that she was as passionate about as Roberto was about his work.

"We should be going," his grandmother said. And then she turned to Stasia. "It's so good to see you again. I hope we'll get a chance to speak more this evening at the party."

"But, Yaya, she…she wasn't invited," Roberto said, looking utterly flustered.

His grandmother reached out and patted his arm. "All the details have been taken care off. We'll see you both there."

And then his grandparents strolled off toward the double doors leading to the interior of the ship.

Stasia turned to Roberto before he could say anything. "I don't know about this."

"She's suspicious of us. I mean, if we were really a couple, you'd come with me, right?"

Stasia hesitated and then nodded. "I'm just having a problem thinking of us, you know, that way."

"If you've changed your mind—"

"No. I said I'd do this." Even though she was now having second and third thoughts about what she'd agreed to. But she refused to let Roberto down.

"Forget it. I'll go tell her the truth." When he started after his grandmother, Stasia rushed after him.

"Roberto, don't. I really wouldn't mind attending the party. Those of your family who I've met, I like. And I've always loved big get-togethers."

She really missed her own grandparents and their extravagant parties. They'd always been so much fun, with singing, storytelling and dancing into the wee hours of the morning.

"You're sure?"

She nodded. "I am."

She hadn't been to a party since…since Lukos was alive. A pang of guilt and a dose of pain washed over her. This would be another first for her since he'd passed.

"Now, I'd better go look over the reports for my grandfather. I have a feeling this evening's activities will include a Q&A with him." Roberto started to walk away.

"Good luck."

He glanced back. "Thanks."

Now was her time to run and do some research and reading before she had to get ready for the party, but instead she remained seated. Roberto had her so confused that she didn't know if she was coming or going.

That evening there were no wardrobe malfunctions.

Roberto was disappointed, as the last time had led to such delicious consequences. He told himself it was for the best that they didn't kiss again. It was better for everyone if they remained friends without benefits.

He'd have preferred an excuse to avoid a big, loud family affair. These things always made him uncomfortable.

When Stasia finished speaking with his cousin Gaia, he leaned in close. "Are you ready to call it a night?"

She turned a puzzled look in his direction. "Since we arrived that's the second time you've asked me that question—what's wrong?"

He shrugged. How was he supposed to explain how awkward he felt around his relatives?

"I have work to do." It was the truth. He always had work to do. And there was a report he needed to review about a prospective piece of property.

"It's more than that. You've been unusually quiet this evening. Do you regret bringing me?"

"No. Not at all." He glanced around to make sure no one could overhear him. "You're the only thing that's made this evening bearable."

"What?" Her gaze filled with confusion. "But this is your family. And they're all happy you're here."

"But I don't fit in."

"That's so sad." Sympathy reflected in her eyes.

That was the last thing he wanted. He shouldn't have said anything. "Forget I said that."

"I can't. Talk to me."

He never told anyone as much as he'd told Stasia. There was something about her that made confiding in her so easy. And she wanted to hear what he had to say, unlike some of the women he'd dated who only cared about listening to themselves talk.

Stasia continued to stare at him expectantly.

He cleared his throat. "You probably noticed that my parents aren't here." When she nodded, he continued. "They dumped me on my grandparents when I was young. I used to wonder what was wrong with me that they didn't want me. I was the only one in my large extended family who didn't have an active mother and father. I always felt different, estranged from everyone else. So I spent my youth studying and reading. And when I got older, it was easier to always be working instead of attending family functions."

"I'm sorry." She reached out and squeezed his

hand. Her touch was warm and gentle. It sent a wave of awareness through him.

"Don't be." He shook his head. "I'm used to it after all these years." But it was the reason he held back a part of himself in every relationship.

"Your parents, they're still alive?"

He nodded. "They rarely show up for these sorts of events."

"Gaia is really happy you're here. So are your grandparents." She nudged him. "Maybe you could smile and act like you're having a good time."

Guilt assailed him. He avoided a lot of the family functions. Maybe in the future he would make more of an effort to attend the gatherings. After all, his grandparents weren't getting any younger, and to his surprise, his grandfather was mellowing a bit.

Not wanting to talk any more about his family, Roberto turned to Stasia. "Would you like to dance?"

Surprise lit up her eyes. "I would."

"I have to warn you that I don't dance often."

"I bet you're better than you think."

He shook his head. He knew his limitations.

Why exactly did he suggest dancing? It was obviously a moment of desperation.

To his relief, the music switched to a much slower, romantic ballad. He was a little better at this pace. And then Stasia stepped in front of him. She was so close. His heart beat faster. He wrapped his arm around her slender waist and automatically drew her closer. His heart pounded his ribs. His other hand reached for her much smaller hand, enjoying the feel of her smooth skin touching his.

Her jasmine scent wrapped around him. All the bad memories, stress and guilt disappeared as if in a puff of magic. The only thing on his mind now was Stasia and how much he enjoyed holding her as they moved around the floor. He'd never get enough of this.

All too soon the music stopped as the band took a break. Disappointment assailed him as he released her. His family and friends joined them at a large round table in the middle of the room. The birthday girl was at the center of the crowd. She looked ten years younger than her eighty years. And his grandmother continued to smile as she'd done all evening.

People pulled up chairs until they were sitting

two and three chairs deep. He and Stasia were at the front, across the table from his grandparents. Moods were light and festive as champagne flooded.

"You two looked so amazing out on the dance floor," his cousin said.

"I don't know about me," Roberto said. "I have two left feet."

"You do not," Stasia piped in. "You are quite talented."

"All I know," Gaia said, "is that you two look so much in love. Maybe you'll be the next ones to get married."

Stasia reached under the table and squeezed his hand. He knew she was nervous and he couldn't blame her. His cousin could get carried away at times. But with his grandmother watching them like a hawk, he didn't say a word.

As the party wound down and they made their way to their cabins, they were hand in hand. It just seemed like the thing a couple would do. And he found that he liked the physical connection—being tied to someone else. Even though it was a fake relationship, he liked that they were in it together. It was a confidence that was shared just between the two of them. It was a link he'd never shared with anyone, as he usually kept people at arm's length.

And as hard as he tried to tell himself it was just a blossoming friendship, unlike the cordial relationship they'd entertained in recent years, this was so much different. She was warmer, funnier and livelier than he'd originally thought. In the beginning, she was reserved with people until she got to know them. Like with his grandmother, Stasia had held herself back. But something told him that if she spent much time with his outgoing grandmother it would all change. He wasn't sure how he felt about it.

Because the more Stasia became comfortable with him and his family, the more comfortable he'd get with keeping her around for the long term. And he didn't do long terms. He refused to end up like his parents, who were involved in a relationship, which was supposedly based on love, but they could barely stand to be in the same room with each other for more than five minutes.

But then there were his grandparents. They seemed to have overcome their problems. He couldn't help but wonder if it was because they came from a generation that believed you toughed out the rough times no matter how bad or how miserable. That didn't sound like something he wanted to try.

It was best for him to remain a bachelor, answering to no one and not having to worry about disappointing anyone.

DAY SIX

Split, Croatia

SHE JUST COULDN'T FOCUS.

Stasia sat in her cabin, having to reread the same paragraph three times. Each time she would get distracted with thoughts of Roberto. What was he doing now? Was he regretting their arrangement?

For as much work as she'd accomplished, she might as well have gone ashore. She had to admit, she'd been tempted. After all, there was Diocletian's Palace, with its cathedral and bell tower to explore. But if she kept running off exploring, she'd never devise her five-year plan.

She turned her attention back to the self-help book about finding what truly made a person happy. Because she was frustrated with herself—with her life. It wasn't that she didn't have enough to do to keep herself busy during the day. She had friends to lunch with. She liked to cook—though cooking for one was a challenge. She was also learning to knit. She'd started with socks—funny-shaped socks. And she had a sister-in-law and niece that she could visit. All in all, she had enough to keep her from growing bored, including enough money that she could travel the world. But she felt driven to do something important with her life—something to make a difference.

And then there was Xander to take into consideration. She knew he wanted her to be happy. She didn't think he'd want her to go into business with him out of some sort of sense of loyalty and obligation. Besides, she was fairly certain her brother was just drawing her into the business because he was worried about her and not because he actually wanted her help.

She glanced down at the book in her lap and had absolutely no idea where she'd left off. With a frustrated sigh, she closed the book and placed it on the table next to her chair. So much for reading.

Stasia got to her feet. Maybe some fresh air would do her good. She headed for the door and walked until she reached the sun-drenched deck where there was a light breeze. This trip was not going as she'd planned. She thought she'd have her goals listed out by now. Potential employers all sorted into a list from her favorite to her least favorite. A résumé put together. A five-year plan detailed and ready to go as she exited the ship.

And all she'd done so far was get drawn into a fake relationship with Roberto, of all people. If Xander was here now, he'd have a fit. She couldn't help but smile at the image of her brother flipping out over a relationship that wasn't even real.

Xander didn't like when things didn't go his way. In fact, he didn't take it well at all. Just like when his now wife had turned up pregnant. That hadn't been in his plans and it had turned his whole life upside down overnight.

Maybe that was what she needed. Not a surprise pregnancy. Definitely not. But something to turn her life upside down. Maybe then she'd be able to see the path she was supposed to take in life. Why did she feel like the answer was just out of her reach?

"What's the matter?" asked a male voice.

The familiar voice drew her from her thoughts. She stopped walking and found Roberto sitting at a nearby table with his laptop open. How was it that on such a large ship they kept running into each other?

If she believed in signs, she would think this was one. But of course, neither of them was interested in starting anything. She wasn't even convinced that Roberto was thrilled with the idea of her being his fake girlfriend.

"Hey," she said, trying to sound happy. "What are you up to?"

"Working on that project for my grandfather."

"I won't keep you." She started to walk away.

"Don't go."

She turned back to him. "I don't want to disturb you."

"You won't be. I'm stuck. So maybe a distraction will do me some good."

He wasn't the only one spinning his wheels. Since she couldn't concentrate on her planning, maybe she could help him. She wasn't sure what she could do, but she was willing to be a sounding board while he talked through his thought processes. Perhaps that would give him some new ideas.

She moved to the seat across from his. "What are you working on?"

"Spreadsheets. Itemized income and expense statements."

That didn't sound very interesting, but there was obviously something of importance in those numbers or his grandfather wouldn't have him going over them. "And does anything jump out at you?"

"No. That's the problem." He leaned back in the chair. "I thought something was wrong and that's why I was asked to look at them. But nothing seems to be out of place." He sighed. "My grandfather didn't tell me what he suspected because he didn't want to influence my findings. Is it possible I'm on a fool's errand?"

"Your grandfather doesn't seem like the type to waste another person's time with looking for a problem that doesn't exist. And if he wanted you to know how well the company was doing, I'm sure he would have come straight out and told you."

Roberto raked his fingers through his dark hair, giving it a tousled look. "Then I don't get it. On the surface, the numbers all add up."

"Then maybe you have to look beneath the surface."

He stopped and looked at her for a moment.

"You make a good point. I started with the consolidated report. I figured it would give a full overview of the business. But there are some other files. They have the backup information. The very detailed information. But it would take days for me to comb through. And I don't have that much time before the end of the cruise."

"You seem to like what you're doing. Do you miss working at your family's business?"

He shrugged, not answering the question one way or the other. "I should get back to work."

Since she wasn't having much success with her five-year plan, why not help Roberto? She could see how important this was to him.

"I could help you," she said, not sure he would take her up on the offer.

He arched a dark eyebrow. "You don't want to waste your vacation combing over reports."

"But I want to help you. And between the two of us, maybe we can find whatever it is your grandfather thinks is important." She paused. Maybe he was just trying to turn her down gently. "Unless, of course, those are secret files."

He shook his head. "I mean yes, they are confidential. But I trust you. I just hate having you do something so boring."

"You aren't making me do anything. Remember, this was my idea."

"Thank you. I don't know what I'd do without you on this trip."

His words filled her chest with warmth. Maybe he did want her around...just as much as she wanted to be around him.

"Wait here. We might as well work outside on this gorgeous day. I'll just run and get my laptop." She stood. "I'll be right back."

She had no idea what they'd be looking for on those spreadsheets. But she liked being able to help Roberto. It felt good to be needed. Everyone needed to be needed sometimes. And it'd been a long time since she was needed.

A few hours later, the answer was still elusive.

He knew what the problem was... Stasia.

Roberto was good at business. He was avid with spreadsheets. And he was great at numbers. But for the life of him, he couldn't come up with the reason his grandfather had him going over these reports. There was something lurking in the figures. He was certain of it.

But every time he stared at the numbers for more than a minute or two, his mind strayed to the dark-haired beauty who for the duration of this cruise was his fake girlfriend. And the biggest problem he was having was that he was enjoying their time together. He was curious to see what it'd be like if they were truly dating.

He halted his thoughts. Was that what he really wanted? Because Stasia was nothing like the other women who had passed through his life. Those women had known up front not to expect anything long-term from him. They knew he didn't do commitments—aside from the business kind. And he never ever uttered the *L* word.

He remembered how his parents would banter around the word *love* as he was growing up. They loved his art projects from school. They loved his grades. They loved how well he did on the polo team. They loved him. And then they were gone. As soon as the school holiday was over, they jumped on their respective flights and headed who knew where. If that was love, he wanted no parts of it.

It was like his parents used the word to make up for being absent in his life. They seemed to think if they said it enough times it would make up for everything. It didn't. It never would.

And so the *love* word had become meaning-less to him.

"Hey, did you find anything?" Stasia's voice drew him from his thoughts. When he shook his head, she said, "I've found something but I don't know if it'll mean anything to you. It's probably nothing."

Considering he still had no clue what his grandfather suspected was wrong, he was will-ing to look at just about anything. He got up and moved to her side of the table. "Let me see."

"It's this." She pointed to a number on the screen. "I can't tell if it's just a transposed num-ber."

She had two screens open at once. One was the consolidated file and the other was the backup information. The consolidated file was supposed to draw from the detailed files, but perhaps his grandfather didn't have the links automated. It seemed a bit odd to him because everything at Roberto's office was monitored with oversight controls.

He checked the next number. It tied to the orig-inal file. As did the next one. Maybe it was, after all, just a typo.

"Can you make a notation of the number,

where you found it and the information from the source document?"

"So it's something?" There was a hopeful note in her voice.

"It's definitely wrong. But the numbers surrounding it appear to be correct. So I'm not sure yet. But it's worth noting."

"Would your grandfather really pick up on a nine-dollar difference?"

He didn't think so. That would be something for the accountants to hash out. But he didn't think they'd escalate nine dollars to his grandfather's attention. There had to be more.

"I think we're still missing something." A big something.

"I'll keep combing through the numbers," Stasia said.

He appreciated how dedicated she was to helping him. She was easy to work with and she didn't ask too many questions. In fact, he was thinking of asking her to come work with him.

Then Stasia would always be close. He wouldn't have to miss her after this cruise ended. Because he was quite certain he would. She was so easy to be around. She didn't make him uptight because she wanted something from him that he wasn't willing to give. And she listened to him with avid interest.

He wondered what Xander would think about the working arrangement. He knew how worried Xander was about his sister. Maybe this would give his friend some peace of mind because Roberto would be able to keep an eye on Stasia and make sure no one took advantage of her while she sorted through the aftermath of her husband's death.

The more he thought about this idea, the more he liked it. And if he was able to think of Stasia as a colleague, it would rid him of these other thoughts—the ones about wanting to pull her into his arms and smother her lips with kisses before tumbling into bed.

Yes, this plan to offer her a job was much better.

"Oh, no." Stasia's voice filled with worry.

"What's the matter? Did you find another mistake?"

She shook her head. "It's not that. It's the time. If I'm going to be ready for us to meet up with your cousin and her fiancé for dinner, I have to start now. And I haven't finished reviewing the report you gave me. There were just so many numbers and the trail back to the source documents can be quite lengthy."

He was having the exact same problem. There was nothing fast about this analysis. And he had a feeling his grandfather knew it.

"I think what you discovered will be enough for today," Roberto said.

"You do?"

He nodded. "My grandfather is a very wise man. He knows it'll take more than an afternoon to uncover whatever it is he thinks is amiss in these reports. That's why he gave me until the end of the cruise."

"Which isn't that far off."

Her concern touched him. "Don't worry. It'll all work out."

"If he asks about it, what will you tell him? Will you mention the typo?"

"I'll tell him enough to let him know we're on track."

She shook her head. "You shouldn't mention me. He didn't ask us both. He wanted you to work on this. Alone."

Perhaps she was right. He didn't like taking credit for someone else's work, but if she accepted his business proposal, he knew this would never happen again.

And so he sent her off to get ready for the dinner. He wouldn't take nearly as long to prepare. It was only after she'd gathered her things and headed for the door to the interior of the ship that he realized he hadn't asked her to be his official assistant.

He'd turned to find her disappearing through the doorway and then she slipped out of sight. The question would have to wait for later. He just hoped it would be the answer she was searching for as far as her future. He knew she didn't have to work. Her family and husband had made sure that she would be well cared for, but he understood the need to have a goal in life, a reason to get out of bed in the morning.

But he didn't want to rush things. He was not a man to be rushed into things. His normal way was to let it simmer at the back of his mind as he weighed the pros and cons of such a decision.

Though part of him was certain they'd make a good match, the other more cautious part of him said to rush things was an opportunity to make a mistake. And a mistake might lead to Stasia getting hurt. And that could not happen, not on his watch.

Perhaps it was best to give it some more thought. Maybe once this project was complete, he would know for sure just how well they worked together.

He decided to work a bit longer on the reports. Who knew what he'd find, but his curiosity was piqued now. Thanks to Stasia.

"Roberto." It was his grandmother's voice. He turned to find her headed toward him. She wore a serious expression. "I've been looking for you everywhere."

He thought of mentioning that she could have called his cell phone, but he refrained. "Now that you've found me, what can I do for you?"

"I'd like you to walk with me back to my cabin."

He turned back to his computer. He thought of telling her he was busy working on the project for his grandfather—

"Whatever you're doing can wait," she said in a firm tone. "This can't."

That got his full attention. He gathered his things and walked with her. She made idle chitchat about the cruise and the upcoming wedding. All the while, he wondered what was really on his grandmother's mind.

If it had something to do with Stasia, he would have to stand up to his grandmother and put a halt to her meddling—easier said than done. His grandmother was fiercely strong and he loved her dearly. But it was saying something when he was more worried about a meeting with his grandmother than he was with fourteen lawyers and a shrewd billionaire.

He paused outside her cabin door and took a deep breath. He sensed his grandmother had something serious on her mind. And that was never a good thing.

"Come in," she said. "Don't loiter in the hallway."

He stepped inside and closed the door behind him. Her suite was the most luxurious and spacious on the ship. She moved to sit at the head of the dining room table where a teapot and service were awaiting her.

She held a cup of what he presumed was her favorite tea. "Would you like some?"

He shook his head. Anxious to get this over with, he asked, "What did you want to discuss?"

She poured him a cup of tea anyway and then waved for him to have a seat next to her. "We need to talk."

He took a seat. Normally, he wasn't a fan of tea, but right about now, he welcomed the fact that he had something to do with his hands. He stirred in some sugar and waited quietly for his grandmother to have her say.

She leaned back in her chair. "You know I'm not easily fooled." His gaze met hers but he remained quiet and she continued. "I know you were not happy that I invited some young women on the cruise to attend the wedding—and for you to meet."

"You shouldn't have done that, Yaya." It was time to make some things clear with his grandmother. "When or if I decide to settle down, I am quite capable of finding my own wife."

Her knowing smile broadened. "Are you ready to admit that you're not really involved with Ms. Marinakos?"

"Why do you presume it's all a pretense?" The truth was he did feel something for Stasia. However, he was reluctant to examine those feelings too closely.

"Because you told me very bluntly that you

were a confirmed bachelor. Why should I believe you are suddenly involved with this young woman?"

"It isn't sudden. I've known Stasia for a while now. She's Xander's younger sister. And she's been involved with the business."

His grandmother's eyes widened. "So you're saying you've been seeing her for quite a while?"

He paused. It all depended on what she meant by "seeing." He'd spent quite a bit of time with Stasia since her husband passed away. Xander had been trying to get Stasia started in his business, and when he was preoccupied with working things out with Lea, Roberto had strived to make Stasia feel welcome.

"What is this inquisition all about?" He cut to the chase. "If you want me to end things with Stasia, it's not going to happen."

He surprised not only his grandmother but himself with such a declaration. The fact it was true was all the more startling. He didn't want this thing with Stasia to end.

His grandmother's gaze widened. "So you're telling me you care about this woman?"

He nodded. It was true. But caring was different than loving someone. He was a long way from that.

His grandmother's gaze searched his. "In that case, I have something for you."

She reached over and pulled a small black velvet box from her purse. She placed it on the table and pushed it toward him. The box sat there in front of him like some ominous apparition.

"Go ahead and open it. It won't bite you."

He had a feeling it would do much worse. He knew what was in the box without opening it.

His grandmother was calling him out on his story. She was going to make him prove his commitment to Stasia. Could he do something like that?

He reached forward and took the box in his hands. He pried it open and found a stunning diamond ring inside set in white gold. His first thought was that it would look perfect on Stasia's delicate hand. And the next thought was that he was in trouble—very big trouble.

He tried to form words to say something and utterly failed. There was a disconnect between his shocked mind and his dry mouth. He sat quietly staring at the dazzling ring.

"That belonged to your great-grandmother. My

mother. I've been saving it all these years and now I want you to have it. I want you to give it to the woman who you pledge your heart and life to." She glanced at her wristwatch. "Look at the time. I have to go meet your grandfather."

And with that, they parted ways. He slipped the ring box in his pocket. It felt like it was burning a hole through his clothes. He'd had absolutely no idea that his grandmother had been saving this for him.

Part of him was touched that his grandmother entrusted him with a family heirloom, but another part of him was angry that she had his life planned out for him. His grandmother had this ring and this ship full of women because she was bound and determined he should be married because it was the way things were done—even though he'd told her marriage wasn't for him. It obviously wasn't for his absent parents either and look where that had gotten them.

And then there was his grandfather with this problem that needed to be solved. Was there a problem? Or was his grandfather trying to lure him back into the family business?

Roberto got the distinct impression that he was

being played. And he didn't like it one little bit. And the more he thought about it, the less guilty he felt about his fake engagement.

DAY SEVEN

Venice, Italy

WHY HAD HE worked so late?

Today there was no room for tiredness.

This was their first day in Venice. And most important, it was Stasia's birthday.

After a cold shower and two espressos, Roberto was feeling so much more like himself. And he couldn't think of anything he wanted to do more than to make Stasia smile. When she was happy, her radiance lit up everything in her orbit, including him.

He'd wanted to throw her a party with all the trimmings, but she'd firmly refused. He would have to do something low-key, but that didn't mean it couldn't be special. And he had the perfect thing in mind. He was keeping it a surprise.

They weren't the only ones going ashore. The ship practically emptied at this stop. He glanced over at Stasia. She was beaming with anticipation.

"Where are we going?" Stasia watched as some passengers went one direction while Roberto took her hand and headed in the opposite direction. "Roberto?" She dug her heels in and they came to a stop. "I'm not going any farther until you speak to me."

He turned to her with a smile on his face. "Do you want to hit a couple of the highlights with a paid tour or do you want to have the most amazing day?"

Like that was a hard question to answer. "Of course I want to have an amazing visit. This is my first time in Venice."

"But it's not mine." Sure, he'd been here for business purposes, but he'd never had anyone to share the magic of this very special city. "I want to show you around. I want your birthday to be memorable."

She removed her hand from his hold. "You don't need to do that. It's too much."

Was she making a point that, since he wasn't truly her boyfriend, he was overstepping? The thought didn't sit well with him.

During the past week, it felt like they'd moved beyond friends. But where did that leave them?

He wasn't sure of the answer and now certainly wasn't the time to evaluate it.

"Relax," he said. "It's just one friend showing another a good time on your birthday. Nothing more." When he saw the worry disappear from her eyes, he said, "We need to catch a vaporetto."

"What's that?"

"It's like a floating taxi."

"Oh."

He reached out to take her hand again but caught himself and lowered his arm to his side. He took off again with rapid steps. When he noticed her lagging behind, he slowed down for her.

The water taxi was crowded as it chugged down the Grand Canal. But Roberto was able to claim the last two seats in the open prow, which provided a sweeping view of the majestic canal. There wasn't much room. When he sat down, his thigh rubbed against Stasia's. A bolt of attraction shot through him, settling in a tightness in his abdomen.

He willed away the unwanted sensation. He attempted to put some space between them but that only succeeded in rubbing not only his thigh but also his shoulder against her. He was becoming increasingly aware of her—of wanting her—in a much friendlier manner than was appropriate. He stopped moving.

"Are you all right?" Stasia asked.

"I'm fine." He was anything but fine. However, that was his problem, not hers.

"I could stand."

As she started to get up, he reached out to her. "No. Stay where you are."

And then realizing he was touching her, he withdrew his hand. She settled once again, next to him. Why had he thought being "just friends" was going to be easy?

It didn't help that this ride seemed to go on and on. There were a few stops along the way before they finally exited at the Rialto Bridge, one of the oldest bridges that spanned the Grand Canal.

Stasia snapped photo after photo on her smartphone. All the while, she wore a big smile that made her eyes twinkle with happiness. Thankfully, his uneasiness hadn't ruined her good mood. The more she smiled, the more relaxed he became. He could just stare at her for hours. It was then that she turned to him and snapped his photo.

"I hope you don't mind. I couldn't resist," she said. "You smile so little when you're conducting business, which is when I see you the most. But on this trip, I've seen a new side of you. The relaxed, fun side of you."

"And this new side, do you like it?" His breath hitched as he waited for her answer.

"I do." Her gaze caught and held his a little longer than necessary. "I like it very much."

"Then I'll make a point of relaxing more often." So long as he maintained a respectable distance between them.

"And don't forget about having fun. The smile on your face looks good on you."

He didn't think her admission would affect him one way or the other, but her words zeroed in on his chest and a warm sensation filled it. She had a way of sneaking past his best-laid defenses. His smile broadened.

They meandered around until they came to the Campanile di San Marco, where they took the elevator to the top of the bell tower. Stasia continued making the pictorial history of their outing. And he had to admit the view from the top of the bell tower was awe-inspiring, with all the historic architecture, but the most amazing view of all was the look of awe reflected on Stasia's face.

With so much to see, they didn't linger long. They hurried to nearby Saint Mark's Basilica, with its most amazing mosaics. And then they were off to the Doge's Palace, where they arrived early enough to tour the hidden rooms followed by a tour of the public rooms. There was just so much history in this amazing city that it was hard to take it all in.

But he had to admit it was so hard to concentrate on the historical artifacts and the culture when the most amazing person was right next to him and all he could think about was pulling her into his arms and kissing her. But completely impossible. He'd promised her they would tour the city as friends—nothing more. It was best for both their sakes.

They shared lunch at an outside café serving authentic Venetian fare, as Stasia insisted they soak up as much of the culture as possible during their brief visit. Stasia chose spaghetti *alle vongole* and he chose to go with a rice dish, *risi e bisi*. And with witnessing her bubbly enthusiasm, he was incapable of denying her just about anything. Seeing Venice through Stasia's eyes was like seeing it for the very first time.

And for dessert, he surprised her with glasses

of prosecco as well as some tiramisu. Her face lit up with happiness and he'd never experienced such joy just by watching someone smile.

"Roberto, what have you done?"

"It's your birthday. We have to celebrate."

"But I told you not to make a big deal of it." But the twinkle in her eyes let him know she wasn't upset with him.

He wasn't well versed at buying birthday gifts, so he'd called his assistant for some advice. She'd assured him that jewelry was the way to go and the salesperson at the jewelry store at one of the ports had concurred. Now that he was sitting here with Stasia, he hoped they'd been right.

He reached in his pocket and pulled out a small box. He placed it in front of her. "Happy birthday."

Her eyes widened.

When she didn't move to take the box, he worried that he'd done the wrong thing. "Don't you want it?"

She nodded, then opened the box. Inside were diamond-and-blue-sapphire earrings. For a moment, she didn't say a word and his body tensed. He'd messed up. She didn't like them.

"If you don't like them, I can exchange them."

"They're gorgeous." Stasia looked at them in awe. "And way too extravagant."

When she attempted to hand them back, he frowned at her. "Weren't you taught that it's not polite to return birthday gifts?"

"Then what am I supposed to do with them?"

"That's a silly question. Put them on."

Her mouth gaped slightly. And then to his surprise, she took off her earrings and put on his gift. Talk about dazzling—the woman, not the earrings. No wonder his thoughts and vision kept straying back to her succulent lips.

He forced his gaze back to her earlobes. "The earrings are almost as pretty as the birthday girl."

She flushed and glanced away. "Thank you."

"You are quite welcome."

The afternoon they spent meandering through the Rialto Market, where a kindly older woman offered to take their photo.

Roberto tried to bow out. Having his photo taken wasn't his thing. But when Stasia pleaded with him, sticking out her bottom lip, he turned to putty in her hands. He moved to her side.

The woman held up Stasia's phone. "Closer together."

He hesitated. Stasia inched toward him, still leaving a little space between them.

The woman lowered the camera and frowned. "Closer."

He stifled a groan. This woman had no idea how hard she was making this for him. Stasia moved until their shoulders brushed together.

The woman still didn't take the photo. *"Bacio! Bacio!"*

Suddenly someone stepped up next to the woman and joined the woman in chanting *bacio*. They wanted them to kiss. Other people in the market added their voices.

Roberto grew uncomfortably warm. He resisted the urge to undo a button on his shirt. What had gotten into these people? Didn't they have anything better to do than to torture him?

Stasia leaned close, making his heart race. She said in his ear, "I think she's planning to hold my camera hostage until we, um, you know..."

"Kiss?" His voice rose a couple of octaves.

Color filled Stasia's cheeks. "Yes, that."

Somehow her discomfort with this whole scenario eased his own uneasiness. "Do you really need your phone?"

She gave him an *are you serious?* look. "Yes."

His gaze moved to the woman holding the phone. She arched an expectant brow at him. "It looks like we really don't have any other choice. If we don't kiss, we'll have to get you a new phone."

"What?" Stasia blinked a couple of times as though processing his answer. It obviously wasn't what she'd been expecting. "But, no, we can't. I have all my photos on there. And my contacts. My life is on that phone."

"What you're saying is that it's important? So important you'd do almost anything to get it back?"

She frowned. "I can't leave here without it."

"What do you want me to do?"

"Just do it."

"Kiss you?"

"Yes."

It certainly wasn't the response he'd been hoping for. Not taking time to consider all the reasons this was a bad decision, he dipped his head and claimed her soft, pliable lips. The chanting stopped and a silence fell over the crowd. He'd only meant it to be a brief kiss, but once he felt her mouth pressing to his, thoughts of pulling away escaped him.

As Stasia's lips opened to him, he was utterly and totally caught up in the moment. The fact they had an audience also slipped from his thoughts. He could only think about the woman who was now in his arms. She was definitely not as immune to his kisses as she had let on.

He drew her closer. His mouth moved over hers, slowly at first, as he didn't want to scare her away. Because there were so many ways this kiss was wrong. And yet nothing had ever felt so right. It was as though Stasia had been made to be right there in his arms.

Her hands slid from his shoulders and wrapped around his neck. A deep moan of longing and excitement swelled in his throat. Could she hear him? Did she know how much he wanted her?

And then the sound of applause broke through his hazy thoughts. Bit by bit, reality came back to him, from being in the market to the woman taking their photo to the growing audience. Audience? He pulled back.

Stasia's eyes blinked open. She looked at him with confusion reflected in her eyes. Apparently, he wasn't the only one to be caught up in the moment. He refused to contemplate what that should mean to him.

The older woman stepped up to them with a big smile on her face. She went to hand Stasia the phone, but Stasia didn't reach out to take it.

"You didn't take the photo yet," Stasia said.

"Oh, but I did. In fact, I took more than one." The woman placed the phone in Stasia's hand. "You two are going to have an amazing future together."

"But we're not together," Stasia said too late.

The woman had disappeared into the crowd. In unison Roberto and Stasia stared at her phone. There was a photo of them kissing. Not just kissing but getting utterly lost in the moment. If he didn't know better, he'd swear they looked like they were lovers—like they were head over heels in love. But of course that wasn't the case.

The crowd dispersed and Stasia slipped her phone in her purse. Neither said a word about the photo. And Roberto fought the urge to ask her to send him a copy of the photo. It shouldn't mean anything to him, but for some reason it did. It was best he didn't have a copy. Otherwise, the only thing he'd get done would be staring at the photo.

"How about some gelato?" Roberto gestured

to a gelato shop. He needed something to cool him down after that rousing kiss.

"I don't know. We just had that delicious lunch."

"But it's your birthday. You're allowed to indulge."

Buzz. Buzz.

"Do you need to get that?" Stasia asked.

"It can wait."

Surprise reflected in her eyes. "But you didn't even check to see who the message is from."

"It can wait. But celebrating your birthday can't wait."

She smiled brightly as she continued to stare at him.

Starting to feel self-conscious, he ran a hand over his mouth. Perhaps her lip gloss had rubbed off on him. "What? Do I have something on my face?"

She shook her head. "Maybe there's hope for you."

"Hope?"

"To learn that there's more to life than work."

As they entered the small shop, he couldn't stop thinking about his conversation with Stasia.

He grew uncomfortable with her peeling back his layers and figuring out how he ticked.

Wanting to change the subject, he said, "It's your turn to order."

She ordered *limone* and let Roberto have a taste of the lemon indulgence. In turn, he shared some of his *gianduja*, with its creamy chocolate and hazelnut flavors.

As they ate, Roberto couldn't help thinking how Stasia's presence in his life made everything feel so different. Until this point, he'd traveled all over the world but he'd never slowed down long enough to savor the gelato. But with Stasia next to him, he wanted to slow down and take in everything about this marvelous day.

When they'd finished, Roberto removed another small box from his other pocket and placed it in her hand.

Her eyes grew wide. "Roberto, this is too much."

"No, it isn't. I don't have anyone in my life to do these things for. Please indulge me."

She opened the box and gasped. "It's gorgeous." Her gaze met his. "You do know that you're spoiling me."

"What can I say? I like to make you smile."

When she went to put on the necklace, she had

a problem with the catch. His instinct was to help her, but he hesitated. Getting close to her so soon wasn't a good idea. But when her frustrated gaze met his, he moved into action.

She swept her hair out of the way and tilted her head to the side. The nape of her slender neck was right there just begging him to press a kiss to it. His jaw tightened as an inner war waged within him.

None too soon, he'd latched the matching diamond-and-blue-sapphire necklace. He quickly stepped back as though sprung from a trap. It fit her perfectly, stopping just above her cleavage. The gems caught the sunlight and sparkled.

"Thank you, again. This is a birthday I'll never forget."

"And it's not over yet."

He'd visited Venice before but he'd never appreciated its beauty. But today, seeing it through Stasia's eyes, it was like he was seeing it for the very first time.

This was such a different side of him.

A more down-to-earth version of him.

Stasia smiled as they continued their exploration by visiting the Accademia Gallery, taking in the great masterpieces. She kept glancing at Roberto to make sure he was having a good time. She never would have guessed he'd be content in an art museum. She knew he was doing it for her and she appreciated it more than she could say.

Lukos never had the patience for this stuff. He was an active guy, from running marathons to playing European football at the park. He always had to be on the go, and strolling through a museum wouldn't qualify.

But Roberto was different. He was interested in what appealed to her. Or at least he'd give the activity a chance.

"This was an unforgettable birthday." She smiled at him. "And it's thanks to you. If it wasn't for you, I'd probably be hidden away in my cabin for most of the cruise. Thanks for being such a great friend."

His gaze delved into her, making her heart beat faster. "I'd like to think we're a little more than friends."

"Does fake girlfriend count?" She was trying to lighten the mood; after the thoughts of Lukos, she needed some levity to alleviate some of the weight on her heart.

"I've never had a fake relationship, so that makes you special."

"And I've never had a fake boyfriend."

"Earlier you mentioned that you wanted to discuss something—what was it?"

"You know how I've been working on my life plan?" When he nodded, she continued. "I see how passionate you are about your work and that's what I want for myself. I want to wake up in the morning with a purpose—one that gets me motivated and ready to hit the day with all of my energy and passion."

"And you're sure that isn't real estate?"

She shook her head. "It's just not me."

"So, what is you?"

"That's the thing—I don't know. I mean, I thought I did at one time. I loved being a wife, and with Lukos's job taking him to many places across the globe, I always had a new adventure. And then we started talking about having a family, but then that dream crumbled. And now I have to find a new dream. A dream that's all mine and not dependent on someone else. Does that make any sense?"

"It does. Do you have any idea what it is you want to do?"

She shook her head. "That's what I thought I would sort out on this trip."

He stopped next to a magnificent marble statue. "And then I interrupted you with all of my family drama. I'm sorry."

"Don't be. I've had a really good time with you and getting to know your family."

"But it doesn't help you find a career."

"No, it doesn't. But I still have the rest of the cruise to come up with something."

"And how's the search going?" There was avid interest reflected in his eyes.

She shrugged. "I know a number of things that I don't want to do."

"Such as?"

"Singing. I can't carry a tune. And I'm not artistic, at all. Though I do love visiting the galleries and admiring other people's work. But I'm lucky if I can draw a decent stick figure."

"Are you considering something in the business world?"

"I don't know."

The more time she spent with him, the more she found she wanted to spend with him. She told herself that she was just lonely. Since Lukos died, her life had become quiet and routine. The only laughter in her life was when she was with Xander's family and her adorable niece.

Now wasn't the time.

Roberto decided to refrain from asking Stasia to work with him. He didn't want to pressure her into a job that didn't suit her. He was certain she would eventually find her way.

As amazed as Stasia had been by the artwork, Roberto was just as amazed by her. There was definitely a deep, abiding strength within her.

She turned a curious look in his direction. Their gazes met and his heart thumped harder. Did she know what he'd been thinking?

Of course not. She wasn't a mind reader, even if she did have a way of reading him quite well.

"You're not even looking at the painting," she said.

"I'm not?"

She smiled. "No. You're not."

"Sorry. I got distracted."

Her cheeks pinkened. "Maybe we should get going. What's next on this tour?"

"Something I think you'll like a lot." He held out his arm to her. "Right this way, signorina."

She smiled up at him as she slipped her hand

into the crook of his arm. And just that small gesture felt so right—as though they had been doing it forever.

There was one more thing burning a hole in his pocket—the diamond ring.

His grandmother expected Stasia to wear the ring, but that would take this charade to a whole new level—

"What has you so quiet?" Stasia's voice drew him from his musings.

"Um, nothing." Nothing he wanted to discuss with her.

Before they could continue the conversation, they'd arrived at the gondola. Roberto turned to her. "Your ride awaits you."

Stasia's face beamed and his heart thumped hard and fast. What was it about this woman that just a smile could make his body react?

Once she sat down on the cushioned seat, he took his place next to her. The ring box dug into his thigh, reminding him that he needed to do something with it. Not now. Definitely not in this romantic setting.

He shifted on the seat, allowing space between them. The gondola was ornately decorated with gold trim and small statues of seahorses. There were red ropes along the sides and fluffy, colorful pillows on the seats. Stasia was quiet as she took it all in.

He hadn't told her but this was his first gondola ride too. In the past when he'd visited this beautiful city, he hadn't felt the urge to ride the gondola. For some reason, it just felt too romantic to ride alone and he didn't have anyone he wanted to ask to accompany him—until now.

Off they went down the canal, gliding over the peaceful water. They took in the striking architecture of the surrounding buildings. They crossed under footbridges and past other gondolas.

His hand moved to the ring box still in his pocket. It dampened his mood. It was like an albatross around his neck. Stasia turned to him with the brightest smile on her face. He moved his hand and returned her smile.

"Are you enjoying the ride?" he asked.

"I am. This is amazing—the whole day has been amazing." She gazed deep into his eyes. "Thank you."

"For what?"

"Making this amazing day."

It had been amazing for him too.

"Roberto…" Her voice was soft as it floated through the air.

Or perhaps it just seemed that way because the loud pounding of his heart drowned out most of what was going on around them. Right now, all he could concentrate on was Stasia.

He reached out to her, tracing his hand over her cheek. "You are the most beautiful woman in the world."

Her lips parted but no words came out.

He lowered his head and claimed those sweet lips. He knew he'd never tire of her kisses. In fact, he was quite certain he would remember this moment for the rest of his life. He didn't care if he got old and forgetful. This would be one of those memories that he would cling to—Stasia in his arms, pressing her lips to his.

As she leaned into him and opened her mouth to him, her arms slipped up over his shoulders, wrapping around his neck. She tasted sweet like the prosecco and gelato they'd indulged in earlier. This was in fact the sweetest, most stirring kiss he'd ever experienced.

A cheer from observers stirred him from the kiss. It was with great reluctance that he pulled back ever so slightly. Stasia smiled up at him—a smile that made her eyes sparkle.

He would never visit Venice again without thinking of Stasia. This was their city.

That was so much better than working.

Wait. Had that thought really crossed his mind? Roberto smiled. He never expected anyone could convince him that sightseeing could be more interesting than business.

Hours later, they walked along the deck. Neither seemed anxious to go to their cabin and put an end to the day. He moved his hand and it brushed over the ring in his pocket. He needed to do something with it. What would Stasia say when she saw it?

Stasia stopped walking and turned to him. "I should head to my cabin, but I want to thank you again for making this the very best birthday." Her gaze caught and held his. "I know you'd rather have been working, but you didn't complain once or rush us at all. That was very kind of you. I'll never forget it."

He continued to stare into her beautiful eyes as his heart raced and his fingers tingled to reach out to her. "There was no other place I wanted to be—"

"Hey, guys." Gaia rushed up to them with a giant smile on her face. "Did you have a nice day?"

Roberto sensed his cousin was up to something, but he couldn't put his finger on what exactly she had on her mind.

"It was absolutely a beautiful day," Stasia said before briefly mentioning some of the places they'd visited.

"Any other news to share?" Gaia probed.

"News?" Stasia sent them both a confused look. "Are you talking about the wedding tomorrow?"

"Not exactly. At least not mine."

And then Roberto realized what his cousin was hinting at. "Gaia, can I talk to you?" When she didn't move, he added, "Alone." He glanced at Stasia. "We'll just be a moment."

They moved off to the side of the deck. Gaia turned to him. "Didn't you ask her? What are you waiting for? Venice is the most romantic city."

"You've been talking to Yaya."

"She told me about the ring. It's so romantic. What are you waiting for?"

He frowned. "I'm waiting for the right moment."

"Can I see it?"

He glanced over his cousin's shoulder to where Stasia was waiting for him. It really had been a nice day. He didn't want to ruin it.

"Roberto?"

"No. You can't see it. At least not now. And don't tell anyone about it—"

"Too late." When his gaze narrowed in on her, Gaia added, "No one said it was supposed to be a secret. You're going to ask her, aren't you?"

He sighed. "Not with you standing here."

Gaia's face lit up with excitement. "Oh. Okay. I'm out of here." She let out a squeal of delight. "This is so exciting. Yaya is going to be so happy."

He pressed his hands to his sides and gave his cousin his most intimidating glare.

"Okay. Okay. I'm going." She gave him a brief hug. "Good luck."

Once Gaia was gone, he glanced around to make sure no other family members were lurking about. The coast was clear.

He returned to Stasia. "Sorry about that."

"What has your cousin so excited? Or was she celebrating her nuptials early?" Stasia hand signaled that Gaia might have been drinking too much champagne.

Roberto shook his head. The time had come. He withdrew the ring box from his pocket and held it out to her. Stasia didn't move as she stared wide-eyed at the box.

"My grandmother gave it to me for you."

"Me?"

He nodded. "And now everyone in my family thinks we're getting married."

"Married?"

He nodded, feeling the weight of the moment. "I think they all have wedding fever because of Gaia."

Stasia's astonishment reflected in her eyes.

He opened the box for her to see the ring.

"It's gorgeous," she said.

"You can put it on." When she cast him a questioning glance, he said, "They already think we're engaged. You should have a ring."

He withdrew the ring from the cushion of black velvet. "May I?"

She lifted her hand. As he slipped the ring on

her finger, he noticed her slight tremble. It fit as though it had been made for her. They both stared at the diamond as it sparkled in the last rays of the setting sun.

"Roberto, what are we doing?"

The earlier happiness and fun had been replaced with tension and uneasiness. "It's only for a few more days."

Her gaze searched his. "I never thought it'd go this far."

"Neither did I. But I don't want to cause a scandal with it being Gaia's wedding. But it's up to you. We can end this here and now."

"I... I need time to think."

"Of course."

She walked away and his gaze followed her. He understood how much he was asking of her. After all, she hadn't signed on for a surprise engagement.

Had that really happened?

Stasia replayed the events of the day as she made her way back to her cabin. She was constantly checking that the heirloom ring was still on her finger.

Roberto had no business giving her something so precious. He should have saved it for the woman he truly loved. And then she realized there was nothing stopping him from doing just that once their charade was over.

Her gaze moved to the ring. This ring was absolutely stunning. The white-gold band had a unique and delicate design. A couple dozen diamonds surrounded a large square-cut diamond. It was fit for royalty—or the woman Roberto truly loved.

The thought of another woman wearing this ring gave her an uneasy feeling in the pit of her stomach. She quickly dismissed the troubling thought.

Once she stepped inside her cabin, she leaned back against the closed door. She closed her eyes and expelled an uneven breath. What was she doing?

Her mind replayed scenes from the day. There were images of Roberto smiling at her and holding her hand. Stasia's heart raced. And then there was the kiss—the very stirring kiss.

Her eyes sprang open, vanishing the thoughts. Instead her attention moved to the diamond ring. It was dazzling. Its setting was so feminine and delicate. It was the type of ring she could imagine being worn by a princess.

But it didn't belong on her finger.

She slipped it off and moved to the bedside table. She gently placed it next to the lamp. Then she sank down on the edge of the bed.

The last rings she'd worn had been the ones Lukos had given her. Her heart squeezed with the familiar pain of loss. What would he think of the mess she'd gotten herself into?

He had been a lighthearted guy. There wasn't much that got to him. That was one of the things she'd loved about him. Would he understand about this? Would he insist on fixing it for her as he'd done for her time and time again? Or would he shake his head and ask what she'd been thinking?

That was a good question. What had she been thinking? She laid her head on the pillow. She'd be helping a good friend who had gone out of his way for her. That couldn't be a bad thing, right?

Roberto wasn't going to fix this for her. He was stepping back and letting her take the lead. Unlike Xander and Lukos, who freely offered their advice, Roberto was trusting her to make up her own mind without his influence.

And the more decisions she made for herself, by herself, the more confident she was becoming in her own decision-making. She smiled. Roberto was helping her more than he knew.

Her gaze returned to the ring. But she still had to decide whether they should continue this charade. If they ended things now, she knew it would cast a shadow over Gaia's wedding. She didn't want to do anything to hurt his cousin.

And if they let it continue, what? Would it change anything? Not really. She'd still find herself being drawn closer and closer to Roberto. And when the cruise ended, so would their relationship. Was she willing to risk getting hurt again?

So what was the right thing to do?

This charade was becoming so confusing. It was increasingly difficult to tell what was fiction and what was real.

DAY EIGHT

Venice, Italy

THINGS HAD CERTAINLY taken an unexpected turn.

She was Roberto Carrass's pretend fiancée.

She picked up the ring, letting the sunlight catch the angles of the many diamonds, sending a cascade of colors over the wall. What should she do?

Today was Gaia's wedding in Venice. And she was Roberto's plus-one. She couldn't think of anyone she'd rather experience a wedding with in such a romantic city—

And then her thoughts clouded with Lukos and Xander. What would they think if they could see her now? She took in her short black dress with the plunging neckline. It wasn't anything too fancy, as she had never envisioned when she'd packed for the cruise that she'd be attending a wedding.

She recalled Lukos's words not long after he'd been diagnosed. He'd made her promise that if he died, she would go on living and not walking around in the shadow that had once been their life.

She hadn't wanted to promise. She hadn't wanted to admit that he might not make it through this battle with cancer. But Lukos had been firm and he wouldn't let her walk away until she'd made that promise.

He'd told her it was easier to make the promise then while he still had his hair, while he could still walk and do most everything he'd done before. It was making the promise later when he was bedridden that would have ripped her tattered heart to shreds. And he'd been right. The end had been—

She shook her head, chasing away the heart-wrenching memories. She refused to let them ruin this occasion.

Even though Lukos had wanted this for her, it still felt not quite right. And she didn't know what to do about that. But every day she was with Roberto, she felt as though she was letting go of Lukos's memory a little more. Not that she could or would ever forget him. He was her first love. But she was starting to wonder if there was room in her heart for the love of two men—

She gasped. What was she thinking? She did not love Roberto. Did not. Impossible. But she was attracted to him. There was no denying that.

And there was her brother to think of. Xander would be furious to know she was involved with his best friend. And she didn't want to damage her relationship with her brother—not for a ship-board fling. Right?

Knock. Knock.

"Stasia, are you ready?" Roberto's voice vibrated through the door.

Her heart raced. Her palms grew damp. This was it. A date.

Not a real date. But it sure felt like a real date. After all, Roberto's family thought they were getting married. And as this charade continued, the lines of their relationship were becoming increasingly blurred.

She was just as nervous as she'd been on her first date with Lukos. No. Correction—she was more nervous.

She tried to calm herself with a deep breath as she slipped on the ring. The harder she tried to calm her breathing, the faster her heart pounded.

Maybe she shouldn't have agreed to this charade. Maybe it was too soon.

But she knew it was just an excuse. It'd been almost two years since she'd lost her husband. She glanced down at her finger where not that long ago she wore a wedding band, which was now replaced with a diamond ring. Would Lukos understand—

Knock. Knock.

"Stasia?"

She swallowed. "I, uh…um, I'll be right there."

She shoved aside the troubling thoughts, along with the reference to love. She was just letting this wedding stuff get to her. That was all.

She gave herself one last glance, making sure she hadn't missed anything. She smoothed a hand down over the skirt. Maybe she should have picked a more cheerful color for a wedding. Maybe the hemline was too short for the occasion.

Another knock drew her from her thoughts. With a sigh, she moved to the door. When she opened it, she marveled at how good Roberto looked. Usually…no, always, he looked so put-together and sharp. But tonight, he looked devastatingly handsome in his dark suit and silver tie.

Her mouth opened but no words came out. Her mind was overwhelmed with how attractive she found him and how much she wished this was a real date.

Roberto's dark brows drew together. "Is something the matter?"

She shook her head. "Um, no. You look great."

"Really? Because you have this look on your face, like…well, I don't know, but obviously you were thinking something."

Not about to delve into how attractive she found him, she turned, grabbed her black clutch purse decorated with tiny crystals and then pulled the door shut behind them. "I was thinking we don't want to be late for the ceremony."

As they made their way through the passageway, he said, "If you changed your mind and don't want to go with me, I would understand. I won't hold you to the arrangement we agreed upon."

It was so tempting to back out. This was her chance. But there was another part of her—a part that wanted to spend the evening with Roberto as his fiancée. After all, when this cruise was over, they'd each be going their own way.

And most of all, she didn't want to let him

down. She'd told him that she'd act as though they were a couple in front of his family and she wasn't going to back out now.

"I didn't change my mind."

He stopped and turned to her. "Thank you. Whatever you want tonight, it's yours. Just say the word. And when you're ready to leave, it's fine by me."

Her gaze met his. "I appreciate that."

They continued to stare into each other's eyes longer than was necessary. Her heart started to race again. Then again, she wasn't sure if it ever slowed down.

He took her hand in his and gave it a reassuring squeeze. "It'll be good having a friend by my side."

A friend? He was reminding her that was all they'd ever be. "Yes, it's always good when a friend has your back."

"Agreed. And I certainly never had a friend who was so beautiful. You've got all of the single guys on this ship jealous that you're with me."

Heat rushed to her face. Where exactly was this evening in the floating city going to lead them? The possibilities both excited and terrified her.

* * *

Roberto didn't know what to do with himself.

Weddings made him uncomfortable. His whole family made him uncomfortable with their expectations of him.

Still, he'd told Stasia that he'd try harder to spend more time with his family and that was what he was doing. Any other time, he would have quietly slipped away long ago. He knew this wasn't going to be easy. But if the smiles Stasia had bestowed upon him throughout the evening were any indication, he was doing okay.

But he'd noticed the sadness that filled Stasia's eyes when she didn't think he was looking. He didn't have to ask her what was wrong; he knew. She was missing Lukos. Her heart still belonged to her departed husband. And Roberto didn't know how to deal with the ghost who stood between them.

Roberto's gaze strayed around the room, searching for Stasia. And then he spotted her, deep in conversation with his grandmother. She appeared to be having a good time.

As Roberto continued to sit alone in the ballroom of an exclusive hotel, he glanced out at the crowded dance floor. His gaze strayed across the happy newlyweds. Gaia had been a radiant bride. In fact, he'd never seen her look happier. He just wondered if it would last. Or if she would end up taking separate trips from her husband like his parents did.

But then he'd watched his grandparents. They were definitely devoted to each other. He'd always considered them the anomaly. They were that perfect couple that everyone dreamed of being when they said *I do.*

Roberto knew what his grandparents had was rare. And he didn't want to change himself, to the point he didn't even recognize himself, to fit in a relationship. If that was what it took to make a successful marriage, no wonder his parents lived apart.

But he didn't want to marry someone just to see them on holidays. That seemed like an impossible situation. The only way he could imagine being happy was to maintain his independence. He couldn't rely on anyone to go the distance with him.

He continued to observe Stasia as she talked to his grandmother. She looked happy now. He wanted her to stay that way.

Part of him wanted to pull her into his arms

and make some new memories with her. But Stasia would expect more from him. She wasn't one of those women who lived in the moment and then moved on to the next man to catch their eye.

Stasia was more grounded. She liked strings and commitments. She didn't take relationships lightly. And her brother certainly wouldn't approve of a fling—even if it got Stasia over the hurdle between her past and her future.

Roberto could almost talk himself into the fact that them getting together would be good for her. It would show her that there was still so much life for her to live. He so desperately wanted to believe what he was saying to himself. And yet he couldn't.

Stasia had been through so much in her twenty-nine years. She was so young and yet she had lived more of life than he ever had. And she'd experienced enough pain and loss for a lifetime.

He wouldn't hurt her. He didn't need Xander to threaten him. He could take care of that all by himself. He wanted to protect Stasia from any further heartache—from the guys on the ship who eyed her up—from himself.

"Hey, what has you so quiet over here?" Stasia leaned in close to speak to him over the music.

He'd gotten so caught up in his thoughts that he hadn't seen her approach him. With her so close, he inhaled a whiff of her jasmine scent. He resisted the urge to close his eyes and savor the scent. But he couldn't meet her gaze either. He didn't want her to read too much in his eyes.

Instead he turned to watch his family out on the dance floor. His family loved to celebrate. The young, the old and the in-between were out there dancing, smiling and having a great time.

"Roberto?" Stasia's voice again drew him from his thoughts. "What's wrong with you tonight?"

"Uh, nothing."

"Really? Because it looks like you're sitting over here frowning and downright miserable."

He toyed with his water glass. "I guess I just don't do well at weddings."

"Are you sure?" There was a heavy dose of doubt in her voice. "You won't even look at me."

He pressed his lips together in a firm line and turned to her. When their gazes met, there was this funny warm feeling that filled his chest. He ignored it as he forced a smile to his lips.

She gave him a strange look. "Really? You can't even muster up a real smile for me?"

How did she know? Could she really read him that well?

"Stop trying to figure out how I know these things," she said.

There she went again, reading him like an open book. He was growing uncomfortable with her being able to sense his thoughts. He'd always thought he was a master at keeping his thoughts under wraps. That was what made him such a good businessman.

He glanced away, not sure what to say.

"You're not that big of a mystery," she went on to say. "You don't want to be here and you regret inviting me."

His head quickly turned. "You would be wrong."

"About what? Being here? Or bringing me?"

"Bringing you. You're the highlight of my evening."

A smile pulled at her glossy lips. "It's about time you admit it."

Wait. Had he just fallen into a cleverly planned trap? If the twinkle of amusement in her eyes was any indication, he most certainly had. Who knew that sweet, innocent Stasia had a much more devious side to her? He was most certainly intrigued.

He held out his hand. "Would you care to dance?"

She placed her hand in his. "I'd love to dance."

This time no words were necessary. He guided her to the dance floor, where he took her into his arms. In fact, the lack of conversation made the dance less stressed and a lot more enjoyable. Except for the fact that Stasia was standing awkwardly away from him.

He told himself that his arms were growing tired with the distance and that was why he tightened his hold on her. But he'd miscalculated, and the next thing he knew, Stasia was snug against his chest. Not that he was complaining or anything.

She tilted up her chin to look at him. Questions reflected in her eyes, but no words were spoken. He'd been mucking up this whole evening and he'd really wanted to give her a good time.

"I'm sorry."

"Don't be."

And then because she kept staring up at him with a look in her eyes that said she could feel the desire that ignited every time they were together, he lowered his head and claimed her lips in what started as a quick kiss, but quickly grew into something more.

Roberto was learning that he would never get enough of Stasia or her sweet kisses. They were utterly and totally addictive.

There was a pat on his shoulder. "Way to go."

Roberto jerked back to find some distant cousin, who was in college, smiling at him.

And then his grandmother passed by him. "Really, Roberto."

His gaze moved from his grandmother to Stasia. He needed to apologize again for losing his head in front of his family. So much for thinking before he acted.

Stasia lifted a finger to his lips. "Don't say it."

He pulled her hand away and wrapped it up in his hand. "How do you know what I was going to say?"

"You were going to apologize for kissing me but I don't want you to ruin the moment. Please."

She enjoyed the kiss? She wasn't upset that he'd overstepped his bounds as a friend—as her brother's friend? What did she think it meant? Was she expecting more from him?

The last question cooled his heated blood. He didn't want her to assume anything. He didn't want to get her hopes up that something more was to follow that kiss.

"Listen, Stasia," he said. When she went to say something, he rushed on. "Don't worry, I'm not going to apologize for the kiss. I enjoyed it too. I... I just want you to know that it was spontaneous—"

"And part of our cover story." She came to his rescue, making this confession so much easier than he deserved. "After all, we want your grandmother to believe we're engaged, so why wouldn't we kiss? It'd be a little strange if we didn't, don't you think?"

How did she do that? Make him go from being totally uncomfortable to immediately putting him at ease. The woman was very good with people. It was definitely one of her greatest strengths.

And so they continued to dance, this song and the next song and even the one after that, which was a fast song. By the end of it, they were both a little winded and returned to their table.

"When's the wedding date?" the bride asked.

He restrained his inclination to frown at Gaia and get her to quiet down. Why in the world would she bring up this subject in front of their grandmother? The woman needed no encouragement when it came to her efforts to marry him off.

"Oh, yes." Yaya's expression filled with eagerness. "Tell us when the big day is."

Everyone pulled out their phones and ran their fingers over them as though preparing to input the wedding date on their calendars.

"We haven't set a date," he said as Stasia's grip on his hand tightened. Apparently, she was feeling as cornered as he did at the moment.

His grandmother looked crestfallen. "I should have known."

"Known what?" His grandfather looked confused.

"Our grandson isn't getting married. In fact, they probably aren't even in a real relationship. This is just an attempt to keep from meeting the young women on the cruise."

His grandmother had read him so well. Was he that obvious? He was between a rock and a hard place. If he disagreed with her, she would expect them to set a wedding date. And if he admitted she was right, then she would have him on a blind date before the night was over.

Stasia let go of his hand and sat up straighter. "It's true. We are serious about each other."

His grandmother's gaze narrowed on them. "How serious?"

Stasia met his grandmother's gaze without flinching. "Well, you know how your grandson doesn't like to do big public displays of affection? He likes to keep things low-key. And so we've been keeping everything quiet—until now."

His grandmother's mouth opened in an O as her eyes twinkled with hope and she clasped her hands together. "So, you are getting married?"

"Yes."

Roberto looked at Stasia. What had she said? He replayed the conversation in his head. Had Stasia really just told his grandmother they were getting married? He opened his mouth but no words would come out. There was a disconnect somewhere between his racing thoughts and his mouth.

Stasia turned to him. "I'm sorry. I know you wanted to keep it quiet for a while, with the transition at your office and all."

"Don't be upset with her," Gaia said to him.

"You couldn't expect her to keep that kind of news to herself."

The next thing he knew, people were throwing around dates. Dates that weren't that far off. And then his arm was around Stasia's shoulders as his whole family debated what date would work best for each of them. He moved and spoke in a dazed robotic motion. Since when was his wedding date up for debate by his family members? Not that he was getting married for real or anything.

When all was said and done, his wedding was set for the beginning of August. His grandmother was over the moon, and Stasia, well, she looked happy. And his family loved her. By the time he found his voice, he didn't have the heart to embarrass Stasia by telling his family that the wedding would never take place.

He knew Stasia had only said those things to keep him from disappointing his grandmother once again. He knew she was even less interested in getting married than him. After all, she'd had her heart ripped out when her husband had passed away. No one would want to risk that sort of pain again. But she'd stepped up, putting herself out there, just for him. No one had gone out of their way for him like she had done. He was truly touched.

"Would you like some fresh air?" he asked, anxious for someplace a little quieter.

"I'd love some."

He once again held his arm out to her, enjoying when she was touching him. And they strolled outside beneath the big, brilliant moon that reflected off the calm water. Apparently, they weren't the only ones with this idea, as there were many couples strolling along the canal.

They walked a bit until they found a stretch of rail where they could be alone. Roberto wasn't in the mood to share Stasia any longer. He couldn't explain it to himself nor anyone else what it was about her that had him rethinking the whole bachelor thing. What had he found so great about it when he could spend amazing evenings like this with a woman who was as beautiful as she was generous of heart?

"Are you thinking about the project for your grandfather?" Her soft voice broke through his thoughts.

How could she think he was pondering work on such an amazing evening? Perhaps he'd had his emotions suppressed for so long now that even she couldn't see he was profoundly moved by this evening, by this trip—by her.

He turned to her, finding her standing closer to him than he'd expected. It was all he could do not to reach out and take her in his arms. But he couldn't overstep again. She'd gracefully forgiven him once this evening. He knew he wouldn't be so lucky a second time.

That thought dampened his mood.

"I was thinking that tomorrow we have one last day in Venice and I was wondering if you would want to see some more of it."

A smile lifted her lips. "I would love it."

"Then it's a date?"

Before he could correct his slip of the tongue, she said, "It's a date."

He smiled. Stasia really did make things easy. He could get used to having her around.

"So I'll meet you on the deck first thing in the morning?" she asked, while staring into his eyes.

"Yes." Resisting the urge to wrap his arms around her and pull her soft curves in for a very long, very deep kiss, he said, "Would you like to return to the wedding? I'm sure it'll keep going until very late."

She shook her head. "If you don't mind, I think

I'd like to stay here just a bit longer before heading back to the ship."

The problem with lingering here beneath the star-studded sky was that he wasn't sure how long his determination to keep his hands to himself would hold out. And he didn't want to mess this up—whatever this was.

He forced his thoughts to the work that awaited him. However, the last thing he wanted to do that night was to work. The thought startled him. He was always up for work. It was his driving force in life—until now.

This trip had opened his eyes. He knew that was a lie. It was Stasia who had shown him what he was missing in life. He wasn't sure his work would ever be enough to fill his life again.

What he really wanted to do was pull Stasia into his arms. He wanted to kiss her without limitations, without his family watching them and without any restraint. He wanted to drink in her sweetness and show her that there was still so much in life for her to experience.

And then he recalled his prior conversation with Xander, promising to watch out for Stasia. Roberto stifled a frustrated groan. Why did Stasia have to be his friend's sister? Because she was the first woman to thoroughly intrigue him. She was the only one to make him question if his permanent bachelor status was really the right choice for him.

DAY NINE

Venice, Italy

Where was he?

Stasia had walked the entire length of the deck twice now, but there was no sign of Roberto. She was beginning to wonder if she'd gotten their plans mixed up in her head. But the more she thought about it, the more she was certain they'd agreed to meet up here.

So where was he?

She tried his cell phone, again. And once again, it went directly to voice mail. That was strange. That man lived on his cell phone. He never turned it off.

The touring party had already departed the boat about fifteen minutes ago. It was too late to catch up with them. And honestly, she didn't want to. She'd been looking forward to her private, guided tour with the sexiest man on the boat.

In fact, she'd had the hardest time getting to

sleep last night and it was all his fault. Every time she'd closed her eyes, she saw his face. And then she would relive the moment when his lips pressed to hers. Even though it was only a memory, her heart would race.

Maybe she was so anxious for today because she hoped he would follow up that all-too-short kiss with a much longer one. Was that wrong? After all, she was supposed to be on this ship figuring out her next step in life.

She knew Xander wouldn't approve of her hitting it off with Roberto. But what her brother didn't know wouldn't hurt him. She knew her brother's heart was in the right place, but she was all grown up and it was up to her to figure out what came next. And who she did it with. Well, if he showed up.

She sighed. Where was Roberto? She sent him a text. And she waited and waited. There was no response to it either.

Roberto wouldn't ignore her, not unless something was wrong. Could that be it? Was he sick?

She took off toward his cabin. With most of the passengers having departed the ship in order to go on a tour, she didn't have to wait for the elevator or have to wade her way through a throng of people in the passageway.

Once she got to Roberto's cabin, she rapped on the door.

"Roberto? It's Stasia."

She waited. When he didn't immediately open the door, she pressed her ear to it. She didn't hear any movement inside.

She knocked again. "Roberto, are you okay?"

Thunk. Crash.

"Roberto? What's going on?"

"Coming."

She breathed easier, hearing his voice. Thank goodness he was safe and sound. Though she had absolutely no idea what had kept him and what caused him to forget that they had a date today.

At last the door swung open and Roberto stood there. His hair was mussed up. His normally clean-shaven jaw now had a shadow of stubble. He was still wearing the same clothes as last night, but they were a bit disheveled just like the rest of him.

"Are you sick?" She'd never seen Roberto unprepared. She'd have sworn he was born ready to take on the world.

He ran a hand over his face and then his hair,

scattering the dark strands every which way. "Uh, no, I'm not sick." It took him a second as though she'd literally just roused him from a deep sleep. He glanced at the time on his wristwatch. "Eight twenty. Oh, no. I was supposed to meet up with you at eight o'clock."

"Yes, you were." She crossed her arms and looked at him. Part of her wanted to be angry with him for standing her up and making her worry. The other part of her was relieved to see that nothing was the matter. Which led her to her next question. "Why are you still in your dress clothes?"

An older couple passed them in the passageway. The woman's eyes widened as she took in Roberto's appearance. And then she turned her attention to Stasia and gave her an approving nod. "Good for you."

Stasia stifled a laugh.

He cleared his throat and opened the door wider. "Come in."

She wasn't sure what to expect as she entered the luxury cabin. Everything about Roberto struck her as him being neat and orderly. But the room didn't appear to be as she would have expected.

Though the bed was perfectly made, there was a black suitcase tossed on top of it. The case was open. Clothes and accessories were strewn across the bed as though he had been in a hurry to get out the door and didn't have time to put things where they belonged.

And then there was the table. It was covered with a laptop, portable printer and tons of printouts. Some of the pages were lying flat on the tabletop and others were crumpled and tossed toward the garbage can but had missed their target.

"I don't understand." She turned a puzzled stare his way. "What's going on? It looks like you worked all night."

"As a matter of fact, I did. Not all of it. But a lot of it." He rubbed his neck and then rolled his shoulders.

"I'm guessing you didn't make it to bed."

He shook his head.

"You work too hard. And too often."

"I'm fine."

Her gaze narrowed in on him. She saw the tired lines etched around his eyes. And the way his broad shoulders sagged ever so slightly as though he were carrying a heavy burden.

Someone had to be honest with him. Someone

had to tell him to slow down—that there was more to life than work. And she knew all too well how fleeting life could be.

She lifted her chin ever so slightly. "You're not fine."

Roberto crossed his arms over his chest as his steady gaze met hers. A muscle in his jaw twitched. "I'm sorry my life isn't to your liking, but it's the way I like it. My work is important to me."

"Even though you're all alone?" She hadn't meant to say that out loud. But she never understood why such a good-looking, successful man would choose to be alone.

His gaze darkened. "Did you ever consider that I like it that way?"

Her mouth opened but nothing came out. She hadn't meant to say that. What was wrong with her?

"I'm good this way. Love and marriage, that may be the way for other people, but it doesn't work for me."

That was one of the saddest things she'd ever heard in her life. "I'm sorry you feel that way because you don't know what you're missing."

His gaze searched hers. "How can you say that after all you've been through?"

"And what? By not falling in love, by not marrying, that I would be better off?"

He hesitated as though realizing he too had said more than he'd meant to. And then he gave a nod.

Was this what everyone thought? That she'd have been better off by never loving Lukos? Well, it was time to set the record straight.

"I am better off for having known and loved Lukos. He showed me how great love can be through the good times and the really rotten, horrible bad times." Tears pricked the backs of her eyes as moments from their life together flickered through her memory. "But I wouldn't trade one single moment I had with him. Not any of it. He helped me to become a better person—at least, I'd like to think I am."

Remorse reflected in Roberto's eyes. "Of course you are. I shouldn't have said that—I shouldn't have dredged up the past. I know how hard this is for you."

"How hard what is?"

He shrugged. "Moving on alone. Mourning his passing."

She wanted to argue and tell Roberto that it wasn't hard, that she was doing just fine. But that would be a lie. It was like waking up one day and having everything you knew about your life and routine being totally altered. It had taken her a while to find her footing again, but she was now able to stand on her own two feet. Now she just had to find a new path to walk down.

"I did mourn Lukos for a long time. He had been such an important part of my life. But I'm moving on now." And then she wondered if she should share her thoughts with Roberto. She wanted to tell someone—someone who wasn't her brother, who thought he had all the answers where she was concerned.

"Do you really think you can do that? Move on, that is?" Roberto's gaze searched hers as though he could see the truth reflected in her eyes.

"Lukos will always have a place in my heart, but he made me promise him that I would move on. That I would have a life and all it entails. And that's what I'm trying to do. It hasn't been easy and there were days when I really regretted making him that promise because all I wanted to do at that point was to wrap myself up in his memories and stay there. But now, well, I'm feeling a little more confident and I know I have to move on, for the promise I made and most of all for myself."

Roberto reached out to her. His fingers gently stroked her cheek. "You are the strongest person I know."

His kind words made her heart swell. "Thank you. But I'm not anything special."

"You are to me."

Her pulse raced and she longed to lean forward and press her lips to his. But perhaps she was reading this moment all wrong. And she didn't want to mess up this special friendship.

After an awkward moment of silence, Roberto said, "I need to get ready for our last day in Venice."

"I… I should go." She moved toward the door.

"You can wait here." He grabbed some clothes from the bed and headed to the shower. "I'll only be a few minutes."

Stasia felt guilty for dragging Roberto away from his work. It was so evident last night that his grandfather was looking forward to Roberto's findings. She remembered her own grandfather and the close link she'd shared with him.

She would do anything to have him in her life again. She missed him dearly.

Stasia's gaze turned to the table with the stack of papers and Roberto's laptop. She felt guilty for coming between him and his bond to his grandfather. She moved to the table and sat down. She had to admit she was curious to unravel the mystery.

Her gaze moved to the bathroom door. It was closed and the sound of running water could be heard. Would Roberto mind if she took another look? She didn't think so.

She opened his laptop and one of the files she'd worked on the other day appeared on the screen. In fact, she noticed that Roberto hadn't gotten much further. She set to work. Maybe, just maybe, she could uncover something more than a transposed number.

"What are you doing?"

Stasia's head jerked up. Her gaze met Roberto's questioning stare with his arched brow. A guilty smile pulled at her lips. She felt like she was back in primary school reaching for a second cookie when only offered one.

"I was bored. I thought I'd look at the spreadsheet some more." As their gazes continued to connect, she said, "You really care, don't you?"

His eyes widened. The color drained from his face. As time passed without him saying a word, she realized how her words might have sounded.

"I meant you care about the company."

The worry lines on his handsome face smoothed. He shrugged, just like he'd done when they'd had a similar conversation. "I've tried to tell myself that I don't care, but the more I work on this project, the more I realize how much I enjoy this business."

"Maybe it's time you went back."

He shook his head as he slipped on his socks and shoes. "I offered to help, but I couldn't work for my grandfather again. We disagree too much."

"Maybe it'll be different this time." She was hoping during the cruise that the two men would repair their relationship—maybe it was too much to hope. "Show me what needs to be done."

"You don't have to do that. I told you I would take care of it."

"I know I don't have to, but I want to." She thought about mentioning how it would please his grandfather to finish this project early, but then she decided to tell him the honest truth. "The thing is, I'm curious. There has to be something here that we're not seeing."

His eyes widened. "You're really that curious?"

She nodded.

"Maybe you found your calling," he said, coming to stand next to her. "Maybe you are meant to be an accountant or perhaps a forensic accountant."

She thought about it for a moment. She did like numbers, but not enough to devote a large portion of her life to it. "I don't think so. I just can't imagine me sitting and staring at numbers day in and day out. But right now, the curiosity is eating at me."

He ran a hand over his still-damp hair. "What about Venice? It awaits us."

She worried her lip. She was torn. Was it wrong that she wanted to do both things?

He held his hand out to her. "Come on. There's gelato to taste and perhaps another gondola ride."

"But—"

"And if you still feel like it when we get back to the ship this evening, we'll work on the reports—together. Deal?"

She liked the idea of working alongside him.

They did make a pretty great team. She closed the laptop and placed her hand in his. "It's a deal."

He gripped her hand as she got to her feet. She expected him to let go once she was standing, but instead he laced his fingers with hers and headed for the door. For the first time in a very long time, she didn't feel alone, even when she was in a crowd of people.

When Lukos had gotten sick, she hadn't noticed it at first, but over time, she started doing everything alone. When he'd been resting, she would grocery shop. When he'd been awake but had no energy, she would clean and cook. As time had passed, she'd grown used to going it alone. She'd forgotten what it was like to be part of *us*.

Roberto was helping her to remember how life could be. And for that she was grateful. And when it was over, she would help him with his project. Together it would be a good day.

DAY TEN

Sibenik, Croatia

EVERYONE WAS HAPPY.

Too happy. And that made him worry.

His grandmother sat across from Roberto at the table in her suite. They'd just finished a light breakfast. And he had yet to learn why he'd been summoned.

His grandmother held up the teapot. "Would you care for some?"

He shook his head before checking the time. He was supposed to meet Stasia soon for another excursion and he didn't want to be late.

"I can see that I'm keeping you," his grandmother said. "So I'll get to the point. I owe you an apology."

He sent her a puzzled look. "No, you don't."

"But I do. When you first told me about Stasia, I didn't believe you. I thought you were dodging my attempts at matchmaking, which your grandfather said would never work. But I watched both you and Stasia over the course of the cruise. I've seen the way you look at each other and the way your face lights up when she's around. I've never seen you happier. And I'm sorry I doubted your love for Stasia. You obviously didn't need my help after all."

Roberto sat there taking in his grandmother's words. She was a wise woman. Had she seen something he'd missed? Was it possible he was falling in love with Stasia?

"Don't let me keep you any longer. I'm sure you're anxious to get to Stasia."

It was true. He was anxious to see her. But did that equate to love?

He hugged his grandmother and left. All the while he wondered how he had let things get so far out of control. He replayed every moment they'd spent in Venice from her birthday to the engagement to dancing with Stasia at his cousin's wedding. He knew he'd never ever visit that city without thinking of her. From this point forward, they were indelibly entwined.

Venice had changed everything for them. First, there had been the photo—the romantic photo—that had led to the kiss. He could still clearly recall the tenderness of Stasia's lips pressed to his. His blood warmed at the memory of her curves pressed up against him.

She'd felt so right, there in his arms. And then as she'd opened herself up to him, it was all he could do to hang on to some semblance of reality.

How exactly had he gone from showing her the sights to giving her his grandmother's ring?

He knew he'd gone a little over the top for her birthday, but there was just something about that day that had him acting out of character, or maybe he should say that he was in character as the besotted lover. He wanted to blame it on the prosecco, but he knew that wasn't the case.

And ever since, they'd fallen into a comfortable companionship that included clasped hands, warm smiles and a mounting number of kisses. But where was it leading? Where did he want it to go?

The walls started closing in on him. He made his way down the passageway, not paying much attention to his surroundings or the people he passed. He kept moving up the steps, through the doorway and across the deck until he was at the rail. He stared out at the water.

He inhaled the sea air, wishing it would clear

his thoughts. But thoughts of their three days in Venice kept replaying in his mind. He should have called a halt to this relationship a long time ago.

And then at the wedding, it was like it had made their engagement official. For all intents and purposes, it was—at least as far as his family was concerned—

Ding.

It was a text message. Roberto was tempted to ignore it, but he knew he was expected to accompany Stasia along with his family into Sibenik today. He wasn't in any frame of mind to put on a show for everyone.

The question he couldn't answer was what exactly did he feel for Stasia? When they departed the boat back in Athens, they'd each go back to their life as though none of this had happened. Wouldn't they?

Ding.

He removed his phone from his pocket and glanced at the screen. It was Stasia.

Where are you?

I've changed my mind. I'm not going.

Then neither am I.

Go ahead. Enjoy yourself. I've got work to do.

I'd rather stay with you. I could help.

Go with the family. They adore you. I'll see you later.

Silence. Then he sent another message.

We okay?

Sure.

Roberto slipped his phone back in his pocket. He started walking. He had no particular destination in mind. Maybe some physical activity would help wear away his frustration.

Time passed slowly. For all of the walking he was doing, he should have gone with Stasia into the city. But he told himself the distance was for the best. Being together day in and day out was confusing things, making this little fantasy they'd concocted seem like reality instead of fiction.

Later, he'd have a talk with Stasia. He'd reaffirm that this thing between them—it couldn't last. There was no way. He was a sworn bachelor. And she was a widow still mourning her husband. And then there was Xander, who would not be pleased about any of this. Definitely too many hurdles for them to cross.

"Roberto?"

He stopped walking and glanced around, not sure who'd called his name. And then he spotted a young woman waving at him. She looked slightly familiar, but he couldn't put a name to the face.

She rushed up to him. "Alone at last."

He wasn't sure what to say to that, so he pretended he hadn't heard her. "Do we know each other?"

She smiled at him. "It has been a number of years, but we used to see each other when I visited my grandparents."

He studied her for a moment. Upon closer look, she did look familiar. It took a moment, but then it came to him. "Little Petra?"

Her smile broadened. "Not so little anymore."

They hugged. It seemed like forever since he'd recalled those days. Petra's grandparents used to live down the road from his. A lot had changed since those days, but so much had stayed the same. It was funny how life worked out.

"Did my grandmother invite you on this cruise?" When she nodded, he continued. "I'm so sorry. She had no right to do that."

Petra shook it off. "It's no big deal. I needed the vacation. But it sounds like you were holding out on your grandmother. I hear congratulations are in order."

"Um...thanks."

She arched a brow. "That doesn't sound very excited."

Petra had been cool to hang out with when they were kids. She always seemed to have her life together and there wasn't any argument she couldn't win. It only seemed natural she would become a litigator. His grandmother had made sure to keep him up to date on Petra's accomplishments and the fact that she was still available.

"I should be going," he said. "It was good to see you again."

When he started to walk away, she reached out to him. "Wait. That's it. You're just going to leave?"

He turned to her. She was still the spitfire he remembered. "Listen, Petra, I have a lot on my mind."

"Let's grab some lunch, and if you want, you can talk to me. I'm a pretty good listener."

He wasn't sure about opening up to Petra, especially about Stasia, but the thought of sharing a meal and reliving some memories appealed to him. What could it hurt?

What was up with Roberto?

Why had he insisted she go on this day trip while he remained on the ship?

The questions whirled around in Stasia's mind as she walked with Roberto's family to the center of Sibenik. The city had that historic village feel, with monuments representing the past and architecture that had definitely been around for quite a while. There was lots to see and learn, but Stasia was having problems concentrating on what the tour guide was saying. And so she finally bowed out of the group, claiming a headache, which wasn't far from the truth.

As she made her way back to the boat, she tried to figure out what to say to Roberto. Everything had been fine until they became engaged. With each passing day, it was becoming increasingly complicated.

Obviously Roberto had second thoughts about

things—about her. After all, she did come with baggage. She was pretty certain none of the other women he'd dated had been widows.

But the thought of him backing out of her life after all they'd shared was unacceptable. She liked Roberto—really liked him. And she thought he really liked her too.

Maybe things had gotten off track. Maybe he was confused about the kiss at the wedding as much as her. If they talked, they could work things out. She was certain of it.

She went straight to his cabin and knocked on the door. "Roberto, it's me, Stasia."

No answer.

She knocked again but didn't hear a word.

That was strange. She thought he'd been in his room working, but then again, it was a beautiful sunny day. Perhaps he'd decided to move to the deck. So off she went to find him.

She pulled out her phone and texted him.

Am back. Where are U?

There was no response. That was odd.

She kept walking and looking around. Surely he wouldn't have gone ashore, would he? No. He was very determined to unravel the mystery of those files that his grandfather had given him. He had to be here somewhere—

And then she spotted him. He was smiling. He was laughing.

Her gaze moved across the table at the café to a beautiful woman who was laughing too. And then the woman reached out to Roberto, covering his hand with her own. The breath stilled in Stasia's throat. What in the world was going on?

Roberto didn't pull away. Instead he leaned toward the young woman and said something that Stasia couldn't hear from this distance. He continued to smile and stare into this woman's eyes.

Something cold and dark churned in the pit of Stasia's stomach. Her body tensed and her hands clenched. This was why he'd blown her off today?

Why did she think he had changed? He was the same playboy bachelor he'd always been. Playing her besotted fiancé must be killing him with all these single beautiful women on board.

Not wanting to get caught staring at the happy couple, she turned on her heels and headed for her cabin. If he was already moving on from the moment they'd shared, then she needed to do the same. She had a career to settle on—a reason to get out of bed every morning—something to fill the emptiness in her life.

And Roberto obviously had nothing to do with her future.

DAY ELEVEN

Bari, Italy

THE FOLLOWING MORNING had come and gone.

And yet there wasn't any sign of Stasia.

Roberto was certain she was upset with him for skipping out on the outing yesterday with his family. He didn't blame her. And if he hadn't been so conflicted about the chemistry coursing between them, he would have gone with them.

He didn't know why spending time with Stasia was getting to him. He was thinking about things that he had no business considering where she was concerned—like pulling her into his arms and kissing her until she couldn't think of anyone but him. And no matter how many times he reminded himself of all the reasons that getting involved with her wasn't a good idea, when he closed his eyes at the end of the day, it was her face that he saw. And when sleep finally claimed him, she was in his dreams warming his bed.

For days, they'd been inseparable, and now she was nowhere to be seen. And it was because of him. She was avoiding him. He'd overstepped with one too many kisses.

He should have respected her space, but he'd thought she'd wanted him too. And when their lips had met, he was certain she'd wanted him just as much as he wanted her.

He wanted to call her, but his phone was dead. He'd checked the ship's courtesy shop, but they didn't have a replacement battery. He'd have to wait until they got back to Athens to have access to his phone.

Having grown tired of pacing in his cabin, he'd moved to the sunny deck. Maybe a bit of fresh air would help him relax. As he took a seat at a vacant table, he heard a familiar voice.

"Good morning." His grandmother placed a hand on his shoulder before passing by him and taking a seat across from him.

"Good morning, Yaya." He slipped his dead phone back in his pocket. "I thought you'd be off on another tour."

His grandmother sighed. "I'd love to, but my body, it's not as young as it used to be. It needs a day of rest."

Roberto nodded in understanding.

"I thought you'd be with Stasia."

"I, uh, haven't seen her since you went off exploring yesterday."

A concerned look came over his grandmother's face. "How strange."

"Wait. Why do you look so worried?"

"Because she left the tour early yesterday. She said she had a headache, but I suspected she missed you." His grandmother's gaze searched his. "So she didn't come back here to see you?"

He shook his head.

"That's very odd."

Concern coursed through him. If she hadn't come back here to see him then perhaps she truly did have a headache. And then guilt assailed him. All this time he'd been sitting around worrying about himself and how the engagement had changed things between them. What if something was wrong and she'd tried to call him? With his phone dead, her call would have gone straight to voice mail.

He got to his feet. "Excuse me."

"Go. Go." His grandmother waved him off. "I hope everything is all right."

He was already in motion before his grandmother finished speaking. He couldn't imagine Stasia needing him and not being able to reach him. As he strode down the passageway, he realized there was a cabin phone. She could have used it to get ahold of him. Unless she was too sick.

Not having the patience to wait for the elevator, he opted to take the steps. He moved swiftly, dodging around the slow-moving vacationers. He had to get to Stasia. He had to be certain she was all right.

When he finally stopped in front of her door, he knocked rapidly. "Stasia? Stasia?" When the door didn't open right away, he knocked again. "Stasia, open up."

The door flung open and there stood Stasia. Her face was devoid of makeup and her hair was pulled back in a messy ponytail. She was still wearing what he assumed were her pajamas—a black cami that hinted at her cleavage and matching satin shorts that showed off her long legs. She looked so good, so very good.

"Roberto, what's wrong? Why did you almost pound the door off its hinges?"

With great effort, he lifted his gaze to her face. On second glance, he realized she was a bit pale and her eyes were dulled. Something was definitely amiss.

"Yaya said you weren't feeling well. I wanted to check on you."

Her gaze narrowed and she didn't open the door enough to let him in. "Would you have noticed if your grandmother hadn't said something?"

"What is that supposed to mean?"

"It means this arrangement is over. Let that woman you were enjoying a leisurely lunch with yesterday, after you blew me off, be your fake girlfriend. I quit." She attempted to close the door.

He stuck his foot in the way, stopping the door. "Stasia, what are you talking about?"

She let go of the door and walked farther into the room. He followed her.

"Stasia, I don't understand."

She turned to him, anger flashing in her eyes. "Don't try to deny it. I left the tour early because I felt bad that you were back here on the ship working hard while I was out having a good time. And imagine my surprise when I find my fake fiancé having a romantic lunch with some beautiful woman."

"You saw that?"

She nodded. "Did you think you were being so sneaky?"

He'd had absolutely no idea that she'd been there. "If you had walked over to the table, I would have introduced you."

Stasia shook her head. "I don't need to be introduced to your lovers."

That was what she thought? That he was involved with Petra? He studied Stasia's beautiful face and the way her big brown eyes reflected her anger and pain. Was it possible their kiss at the wedding had meant something to her? Was she jealous?

"Her name is Petra. And she's not my lover."

Stasia's mouth opened but nothing came out. She pressed her lips together into a firm line as though she was making sense of what he was saying. Emotions flickered through her eyes as reality started to take hold.

Stasia pressed her hands to her hips and lifted her chin until they were eye to eye. "Are you saying you aren't interested in her?"

Roberto couldn't help but laugh. "I think of Petra like a little sister."

"Sister?"

He nodded in affirmation. "She grew up on the estate next to my grandparents'. When we were kids, she played with me and my friends."

"You...you were childhood friends?"

He smiled and nodded.

"You aren't romantically involved?"

He shook his head. "The idea never even crossed my mind. I don't think of Petra that way and she doesn't see me that way. My grandmother invited her on the cruise, thinking there was a chance for something more. She was wrong."

"So if Petra isn't interested in you, why did she agree to come on the cruise?"

"She was in need of a vacation and she is good friends with Gaia. So, basically, she was here for the wedding."

Stasia's eyes widened with hope. "Not you?"

"Not me." He stepped closer to her and caressed her cheek. "The only woman I have eyes for on this cruise is you."

"Really?"

"Really." And he didn't stop to think of the right or the wrong of it; he just acted.

He reached out to her, placing his hands on her slender waist and drawing her to him. And she willingly moved closer to him. He lowered his head and pressed his lips to hers.

For so long, he'd been fighting his feelings for her. But after seeing that she cared enough about him to get so worked up—so jealous—he'd been moved. He'd never had another woman in his life stir him the way Stasia did.

His mouth moved over hers. With the heated emotions, it didn't leave room for a soft and gentle kiss. Instead their lips moved hungrily over each other. Her hands moved to his shoulders before moving to the back of his neck. He'd never get enough of her touch.

Roberto reached behind him and pushed the door shut. He was going to show Stasia that there was no other woman in his life. All he could think about—dream about—was her.

As the kiss deepened, he scooped Stasia up in his arms. He carried her to the bed and laid her down. He leaned down, continuing to kiss her.

But before this went any further, he had to be entirely sure it was what she wanted too. It took every bit of willpower he could muster to pull away from her sweet, sweet kisses.

Stasia's eyes fluttered open. Confusion reflected in her eyes. "What's the matter?"

"Stasia, are you sure this is what you want?"

Her gaze met his. In its depths desire flickered. "I want you. All of you."

And then she drew him to her, smothering his words with a kiss. A kiss that was sweeter than anything he'd ever imagined. How did he get so lucky to have Stasia in his life?

DAY TWELVE

Crotone, Italy

THE NEXT MORNING, before Stasia opened her eyes, she reached out for Roberto. Her hand landed on an empty spot in the bed. Her eyes fluttered open. Her gaze searched the cabin.

He was gone.

She closed her eyes, trying to keep her emotions under control. Why did she think it would be different? She knew about his *love 'em and leave 'em* reputation. Why did she allow herself to believe that he was different than people thought?

She opened her eyes and reached for the blankets. With a big yank, she pulled them up to her chin. That was when a slip of paper fluttered in the air. What in the world?

It landed on the other pillow—the pillow where not so long ago Roberto had been. She picked it up.

Good morning, beautiful! Had some things to take care of before we head off on our next adventure. See you soon. Roberto.

The note should have made her smile. It didn't. The knowledge that their night together had meant more to Roberto than an itch he needed to scratch or a casual fling scared her.

It wasn't the reaction she'd been expecting. The truth was that she'd had no idea how she would react to their lovemaking. She hadn't let her mind jump that far ahead.

He was the first man she'd been involved with since Lukos. For so long, she'd sworn there wouldn't be another man. And now there was Roberto.

She should feel guilty for moving on, shouldn't she? But she didn't.

After all, Roberto wasn't a stranger to her. She'd known him for quite a long time, and while on the cruise, they'd grown close as friends. Still, what had happened went beyond friendship— far beyond it.

Last night, their relationship had been irrevocably changed. Their fake relationship was now a real one. Her stomach shivered with nerves.

Where was this leading? Where did she want it to lead?

She didn't have the answer to those questions. The only thing she knew was that her life had just become even more complicated.

History abounded around them.

But all Roberto could think about was the woman standing next to him.

They'd just toured the sixteenth-century Castle of Charles V. And, if asked, Roberto couldn't tell anyone what they'd seen. His attention was distracted by Stasia's quietness.

He knew their night together had been a huge step for her. He'd been so worried that in the aftermath she'd pull away from him—so worried that he hadn't taken time until now to realize how significant the moment had been for him.

For so long, he'd kept everyone at a distance, but that was impossible to do with Stasia. There was no wall, no barrier that she couldn't scale. She saw through him—straight through to his damaged heart.

He didn't know what to do about it. Stasia had already been hurt so deeply when she lost her husband. Roberto didn't want to do anything to cause her more pain. Or was it too late?

Not liking the direction of his thoughts, he started to talk about his project for his grandfather. It seemed like a safe enough topic.

But after a while, he noticed Stasia's distinct lack of input. "Enough about me," Roberto said. "You've been quiet. Is everything all right?" He stopped and turned to her. "Are we all right?"

She sent him a smile that didn't quite reach her eyes. "We're fine."

He nodded in understanding. It was going to take them both some time to make sense of what was happening between them. He took her hand in his and they began to walk.

"We've talked a lot about me and my stuff—it's time we focus on your future."

"I don't think so."

"You've helped me so much. Now I want to return the favor." He really did want to help her. "If you just need someone to bounce ideas off, I'm your guy. If you need me to make a phone call and pull some strings, I'm there for you. If you need—"

"Okay. Stop." Stasia smiled. "I appreciate your

support. I really do. But this is something I have to figure out on my own."

"I can't imagine that a little help will hurt."

She glanced over at him as they continued to walk around Crotone with no particular destination in mind. "Maybe a little."

"Okay. What can I do?"

She paused as though thinking over her answer. "What career do you think I should pursue?"

The fact she wanted his input touched him. Sure, people wanted his opinion when it came to business—to making a deal. But this was different. This was so much more personal. And that was something he'd been avoiding...until now.

"I can't tell you what to do." When she went to say something, he stopped her. "But I can ask you a question. In your past, when were you happiest?"

They continued walking in silence as though she were giving the question some deep thought. After a while, she said, "That's not an easy question to answer. I did retail when I was a kid."

"Really?" The word slipped out before he could stop it.

She turned to him and frowned. "What? You think I've always been spoiled?"

He opened his mouth but realized this was a trap. Knowing no matter what he said he would be in trouble, he closed his mouth without saying a word.

"Well," she said, "the truth is my grandfather believed in teaching my brother and me what it's like to fend for ourselves."

"Okay, then. Is retail work something that appeals to you? You could open your own boutique."

She tilted her head to the side as though recalling those memories. And then she shook her head. "I don't think so."

"What else is there?"

"I worked in the library in college. And as much as I love to read, well, that isn't for me."

"Keep going."

She sighed. "There isn't anything after that, I'm afraid. Because Lukos and I got married straight out of college. And then he got sick and that took up our lives. Except..."

Roberto stopped walking and turned to her. There was something in her voice. She'd had a thought and something told him that it was important. "What is it?"

She shook her head. "It's nothing."

"It's definitely something. Tell me."

She sighed. "I was just thinking about when Lukos was in the hospital."

"Oh." He'd totally misread her. He didn't mean to lead the conversation in this direction. What had made him think he knew her so well?

"No, it's not that. Lukos didn't want me hanging over him while he was getting his treatments, so I had time on my hands. One thing led to another and eventually I ended up volunteering my time." She smiled. "I met some of the most amazing people. They had every reason to be gloomy and yet they cheered me up. Can you believe that?"

"It sounds like they touched you."

"They did. They really did."

"The way your face lit up talking about them says a lot."

"But I didn't do anything special. I took a cart around the oncology ward. I handed out books, snacks, games, anything to take the patients' minds off their problems for a moment."

"And how did that make you feel?"

She shrugged. "I loved seeing people smile and knowing I had something to do with it. More than anything, they just wanted someone to listen to them."

"Then you have your answer."

"What answer?"

He took her hands in his own. "You are the most giving, caring person I know. When you speak of your volunteer work, your whole face lights up. I think that's what you should do—help people."

"You think I should go back to pushing the cart around the ward?"

He shrugged. "You could do that. Or you could head up your own foundation that would help people."

Her mouth gaped and then she shook her head. "I couldn't do that."

"Why not? You understand people. You're good with numbers. And if you need donors—and you will need donors—I'll be the first in line. Your brother will be the second in line."

Her gaze searched his. "You're serious, aren't you?"

"Of course I am. This world needs people like you—people who are willing to help others in

need. I couldn't think of anything more reward-
ing—"

"Or painful. I've already lost a husband."

He grew quiet. He'd seen how she got excited
over the memory and he'd let himself get caught
up. In that moment, he'd forgotten what she'd
been through. He knew that losing her husband
had been devastating for her. What was he thinking to suggest that she deal with those memories
on a daily basis?

"Forget I said anything." He started walking
again and she fell in step next to him.

She didn't say anything, but he sensed her
thoughts were on that traumatic period of her
life. Here he'd been trying to get her to let go of
the past and focus on the future. And now he'd
undone everything.

The day had gone by way too fast.

And now the sun was starting its slow descent
toward the horizon.

Stasia and Roberto made their way back onto
the ship. They weren't the only ones returning
from a day excursion. All around them people
were laughing, talking and just enjoying the day.

She couldn't blame them; it was wonderful. So was the company.

"Wasn't that beautiful?" Stasia said with a smile on her face.

"Yes, you are quite beautiful." Roberto tightened his arm over her shoulders, drawing her close.

"Today was amazing."

"Last night wasn't too shabby either."

Stasia couldn't believe this side of Roberto existed. Today he was sweet, thoughtful and fun. As they'd toured the ruins around Crotone, he'd been a different man. From him suggesting they pose in front of the Castle of Charles V for a photo, to taking his time to view sacred parchments, books and icons at the museum. Today there was no rushing around. The fact he was genuinely interested in the same things thrilled her.

Roberto had reminded her that she hadn't died with Lukos, even though it had felt like it at the time. Roberto had let her enjoy herself without the guilt of still being alive while Lukos wasn't. Roberto didn't rush her. He didn't expect things of her. He just accepted her as is.

Stasia moved off to the side of the deck, out

of the way of the returning tourists, and turned to Roberto. He'd been so different since they'd cleared the air last night. She hadn't known it was possible to be so jealous. And it had all been for naught. Thankfully.

"You know, if you're not careful, I'm going to fall for all of your compliments."

Roberto's eyes reflected his playful mood. "You deserve to be complimented every single day and night."

She shook her head and lowered her gaze, feeling uncomfortable with his blatant flattery. "No, I don't."

Roberto placed a finger beneath her chin and lifted until their gazes met. "I mean it, Stasia. You are very special."

And then his head lowered, capturing her lips with his. Her heart pounded with excitement. She leaned into his embrace. It would be so easy to believe this was the beginning of something— something special.

The echo of voices faded into the background. The fact they were standing in a crowd of people while kissing didn't matter. The only thing that mattered in that moment was him and her.

"Roberto."

The stern, disapproving male voice had them jerking apart. Stasia immediately missed the feel of Roberto's touch. She longed to sidle up next to him—to wrap her arms around his trim waist—to lean into him.

Instead she turned to find his grandfather frowning at them. It appeared his grandfather didn't believe in public displays of affection. That was too bad because she couldn't promise she wouldn't give in to her desire to share a kiss with Roberto in public again.

"I'm surprised to find you out here." His grandfather's voice held a note of disapproval. "I've been looking for you. I called your cell but it went to voice mail."

Roberto smoothed his fingers over his mouth. "Hello, Grandfather. My phone died."

When a strained silence ensued, Stasia spoke up. "We just got back from sightseeing. Did you have a chance to visit Crotone?"

His grandfather's gaze flickered to her. "I did not." Just as quickly, the older man's attention returned to his grandson. "I attempted to catch up with you this morning, but it appears you had other priorities."

"I just wanted to see the sights with my fiancée." Roberto reached out and took her hand in his.

His grandfather's suspicious gaze moved between the two of them. "Are you trying to tell me this relationship is real? It's not just a ruse to keep your grandmother off your case?"

"What?" Roberto's gaze moved to her before returning to his grandfather. "Of course this is real. You just saw us kissing."

It was like the sweetness of the kiss had been wiped away and now the kiss was nothing more than part of their charade. Was that right? Was she just getting caught up in the show they were putting on? Or was there a genuineness to what they'd shared last night?

The frown lines on his grandfather's face smoothed. The man turned to Stasia, who remained by Roberto's side. "I'm sorry for interrupting your day. It looks like my grandson makes you very happy. And you do the same for him."

"He does—make me happy, that is." Stasia smiled brightly as though to confirm her words. It wasn't a lie to keep the charade going. It was the truth.

"I'm sorry to intrude—" his grandfather took

on a more serious tone as he turned back to Roberto with a direct stare "—but I wanted to discuss those files with you. I assume since you have time for sightseeing that you've completed the project."

Roberto's body tensed. His grip on Stasia's hand tightened. His grandfather was calling him out for not spending every moment working and it was her fault. She was the one who'd lured him out for a day of leisurely strolls, delicious food and good times beneath the Italian sun.

The tension coursing between the two men was palpable. Stasia's mind raced for something—for anything—that would break the rising tempers.

"It's my fault," she uttered. Both men turned to her and she knew she had to keep going. "I asked Roberto to go sightseeing today. If you're angry with anyone, it should be me—"

"It's not her fault." Roberto gave her a stern look as though telling her to back off—that this was his fight. "I should have stayed and worked today."

Not one to be warned off, she said, "But I promised him that I would help him—"

"Help him?" His grandfather's gray brow

arched. "Is that true, Roberto? Do you need help?"

Stasia inwardly groaned. "That isn't what I meant—"

"Stasia, stop." Roberto released her hand. "You don't owe my grandfather any explanations."

Immediately her lips pressed together in a firm line, holding back all the words she now wanted to say to Roberto. She'd been trying to help him. If he didn't want her help, she didn't know what she was doing here.

Roberto straightened his shoulders. "You didn't say how I was to complete your project. In fact, I don't even have to work on this thing for you."

Now she could see why Roberto had opted to work with her brother. Both Roberto and his grandfather had iron wills. Neither wanted to back down.

"Are you saying you're quitting?" his grandfather asked.

There was a moment of silence as though Roberto was weighing his options. "I plan to work on your reports the rest of the evening. And before you ask again, yes, Stasia is assisting me."

"Those are confidential reports."

"And I trust her explicitly." He turned to her. "Would you mind giving us a minute alone?"

Stasia nodded before walking away. She hoped the two men would make peace with each other. Everyone needed family—whether it was by blood or by choice.

Roberto's back teeth ground together.

Instead of his grandfather being grateful for the help, he could only criticize the way he'd gone about accomplishing it. Roberto remembered exactly why he'd quit working for his grandfather all those years ago.

Once Stasia was out of earshot, Roberto turned to his grandfather. "Don't ever do that again."

"Do what?" And then his grandfather's eyes widened in understanding. "You really do care about her. Your grandmother said it was real. I should have trusted her instincts. She's pretty good at spotting these things."

"Not when it came to my parents," Roberto muttered under his breath.

"That was different."

Roberto hadn't meant for his grandfather to hear him, but now that he had, Roberto had some questions. "How was it different? My parents can hardly stand to be in the room together."

"What you don't know is that your grandmother and I vehemently opposed their marriage. But the harder line we took, the more insistent your parents were about marrying."

Having a very strained relationship with both parents, he would never broach this subject with either of them. "So why don't they get divorced?"

His grandfather sighed. "That's a question I've asked myself many times. And the only thing I can figure out is that they truly love each other."

"No." Roberto shook his head. "I've seen them. They don't touch. They hardly talk to each other."

"But when you see them, they are with the family. They feel awkward and don't want any pressure put upon them."

"And what? They get along when they are off on their own?"

His grandfather smiled and nodded. "Your father told me they've found a way to be happy together."

"But without me."

His grandfather walked over to him and briefly touched his hand to Roberto's shoulder. "I am sorry about that. Not all people are meant to be parents. Your grandmother and I, we did the best we could, but we weren't your mom and dad. And...and I worried that I'd make the same mistakes with you that I made with your father. So I overcompensated by being harder on you. Too hard. I... I'm sorry."

His grandfather's explanation and apology were like a balm on his scarred heart. Maybe there was a possibility for a new beginning for them. He could finally allow himself to admit that he missed his family.

As frustrated as Roberto had been with his grandfather, he loved him even more for always being there—even when Roberto didn't make the choices his grandparents wanted him to make.

"Thank you for being the steady presence in my life."

His grandfather was quiet for a moment. "Maybe this can be a new start for us."

Roberto nodded. He liked the thought of being closer to his grandfather—of returning to the family business.

His grandfather gave his shoulder another squeeze. "I should be going. Your grandmother will be looking for me." His grandfather started to walk away but then paused and turned back.

"Don't plan your future based on your parents' choices. You are your own man and quite capable of anything you set your heart and mind on."

And that was it. His grandfather moved toward the interior of the ship, leaving Roberto to grapple with the realization that his parents loved each other in their own way. Maybe he should have seen this—should have suspected this, but he'd been so angry with them most of his life that he was oblivious.

Even though they loved each other, he would never want a life like theirs. And he knew that Stasia wouldn't want that lonely life either. Not that he was considering truly marrying her or anything.

There were still a few more days of the cruise. And he knew that when the ship made port in Athens this whole fantasy would come to a screeching halt.

He wasn't ready to deal with that now. He had enough on his mind with his grandfather and his looming deadline.

Together, he and Stasia quietly made their way to his cabin. Once the door closed, Stasia asked, "What in the world happened back there?"

"My grandfather was just being himself."

"But he was so kind and friendly before."

"And he was trying to get me to do something for him. Now that I'm doing what he asked, he doesn't have to play nice." He didn't want to discuss what he'd learned about his parents. He was still trying to make sense of it.

Stasia pursed her lips. "Is it possible it was something else?"

"Something like what?"

"Like he's worried and anxious to find out what you've learned."

Instead of quickly rejecting her speculation, Roberto paused. Did she have a point here? He rubbed the back of his neck. "I don't know. I've been butting heads with him for so long now that there's where my thoughts naturally go. But maybe you're right. I do know that he looks more tired than I've ever seen him."

"Is it possible there's more to those reports than a few transposed numbers?"

"I know there is. My grandfather wouldn't send me on a fool's errand. There is something definitely wrong. I can feel it in my gut. But it might be more serious than I originally suspected."

"Or maybe you want there to be something

there for you to find so you can prove yourself to your grandfather."

There she went again, seeing more of him than he wanted anyone to see. "I don't have anything to prove."

"Says the man working at another company instead of his family business."

He stepped up to her. He needed to look her in the eyes when he set the record straight. "I work with your brother because he's my friend and I like what I do. You don't know me as well as you think."

Stasia's eyes grew round as her mouth slightly gaped.

He inwardly groaned. That had come out much gruffer than he'd intended. He didn't want to hurt Stasia's feelings. In fact, that was the furthest thing from his mind.

He just needed her to stop pulling back the scabs on his life's traumas. One by one, she was revealing the real Roberto, and he felt exposed. It was not a situation he was used to finding himself in.

The truth was he never left the family business because he wanted to leave. He'd done it to stop the daily arguments with his grandfather.

He'd never said he wouldn't go back. It just had to be on his terms.

"I'm sorry," he said.

"No. I'm the one who's sorry. Sometimes I forget myself and I venture into subjects that are none of my business." She glanced off to the side. "Maybe I should leave."

He sighed. He was single-handedly ruining this most perfect day. But it wasn't over yet; there was still a chance to salvage it.

"Don't go. I know I took my frustration with my grandfather out on you. I shouldn't have done that."

Stasia hesitated. "And I pushed you more than I should have."

"How about we start over?"

"Do you think it's possible?"

"I could order us some dinner," he said.

"And I could get started on those reports."

"You don't have to."

"I want to."

He smiled and nodded. "Thank you."

DAY THIRTEEN

Sicily, Italy

THIS WAS UNBELIEVABLE.

She was standing on a volcano.

Stasia felt giddy inside. It was exciting to push herself and try new things. A year ago or even five years ago, she would have played it safe. Lukos had been a cautious man. When she'd push for them to be more adventurous, such as going on a weeklong hiking trip along the Amalfi Coast in Italy, he'd countered with a long weekend in wine country in a five-star hotel. She hadn't argued, perhaps she should have, but she'd preferred to make him happy. And the spa at the hotel had been out of this world.

But thanks to Roberto, she was finding she was capable of so much more. He didn't hold her back. He encouraged her to explore—to take chances.

Stasia couldn't believe she was seriously considering Roberto's idea of starting her own foundation. The man seemed to have a way of convincing her she was capable of doing anything she set her mind to. As this trip went on, she was learning that she was capable of far more than she'd previously given herself credit for. She wouldn't make that mistake again.

Still, she worried about letting herself get closer to him. She had to learn to count on herself for her happiness. But as her gaze moved to Roberto, she had absolutely no desire to put any distance between them.

And then his gaze caught hers and her stomach dipped. He flashed her a smile, causing her to smile back at him. If it weren't for Roberto, she wouldn't have thought to challenge herself—to go beyond what she thought were her limits.

"What has you smiling?" Roberto's voice cut into her thoughts.

"You. You have me smiling."

"I do?" His voice came out as an enticing deep growl. He moved to stand in front of her. His hands wrapped around her waist as her hands came to rest on his shoulders.

She nodded. "Standing at the foot of a massive volcano is something I never thought I'd do. I'm beginning to feel like anything is possible."

"You can do anything you set your mind to."

As the breeze rushed past them, she leaned her head back. She stared up at the clear blue sky. She couldn't believe this cruise was almost over. She wanted to make the most of every moment they had left.

It was then that she felt Roberto press his lips to her neck. A shiver of excitement coursed through her body. Apparently she wasn't the only one who wanted to make the most of the time they had left.

When she straightened up, she realized their tour group was getting away from them. "We better hurry across this lava field before they leave us behind."

"Would that be such a bad thing?"

She lightly slapped his arm. "Seriously? And miss the best part."

"The best part?"

She started walking. Roberto fell in step next to her. She moved as quickly as she could, considering they were in a lava field.

"Don't you want to wear a helmet and take a flashlight to explore a lava cave?" She glanced over at Roberto, who was smiling and shaking his head. "What? It sounds exciting."

"Until something creepy and crawly comes out and attacks you."

She visibly shuddered. "It doesn't matter what you say—it's not going to stop me."

"Are you sure? I hear the spiders down there are big. Really, really big. With long, hairy legs and googly eyes—"

"Stop!" She frowned at him. "How did you know?"

"That you're afraid of spiders?" When she nodded, he said, "It was a calculated guess."

"Calculated? Are you saying I'm predictable?"

"I'd never say that. Because I never would have predicted you'd become my fiancée."

She smiled. For just that moment, she wanted to give in to the fantasy, imagine what it'd be like to really be Roberto's true love—his destiny. Her gaze moved to the heirloom diamond on her hand. It was meant for Roberto's wife—the woman he was meant to spend the rest of his life with.

In that moment, she realized that she never wanted to give up the ring. Because to surrender the ring would be to surrender the blissful fantasy. And she didn't want this to end.

The breath stilled in her chest. Her heartbeat slowed. What was she saying? Did she really want this engagement to continue?

And then she knew the answer. It wasn't some mysterious answer that she had to wrestle with. The answer came to her so quickly, so easily that it was startling. No matter how much she wanted to fight it—deny it—she was falling in love with Roberto.

She glanced at the ring again. Ever since he'd put it on her finger, it was like it had pulled the blinders from her eyes. And now she was able to see what was clearly in front of her—Roberto.

He took her hand in his. "What are you thinking about?"

"Um, nothing."

"That look on your face says otherwise. Must be something good."

She glanced at him. "I was just thinking this is such a lovely day."

"It is a really nice day. But I think there's more going on in that mind of yours than that."

She shrugged but didn't elaborate. Some thoughts were best to keep to herself until she decided how to tell him. She didn't know what he'd say. Would he be happy?

What was she saying? They'd just made love. He must feel the same way or he wouldn't be here with her in a lava field about to descend into a cave.

Roberto played his emotions so close to his chest that sometimes it was so hard to read him. But with them reaching the mouth of the cave, it was best to leave the subject alone until they returned to the chalet.

What was going on?

She'd been acting strange all day.

Roberto couldn't shake the feeling things had shifted with Stasia. He wanted to say that escalating their relationship had been a mistake, but he couldn't dismiss such an amazing night. But it wasn't just Stasia who was confused.

And this was why he worked rather than trying to have a relationship. For the most part, his work was straightforward. But this thing between him and Stasia was anything but straightforward. He didn't know what to say or how to act.

At lunch at the nearby chalet, when she didn't think he was looking, she would stare at him.

She didn't say anything, but there was a different sort of energy coursing between them. And it had nothing to do with the fresh air or bright sunshine. Nor did the change between them have to do with the delicious meat-and-cheese tray or the local wine. No, this change had to do with him letting go of his common sense and giving in to his desires. And now he didn't know how to rewind the clock.

"You're awfully quiet," Stasia said as they made their way onto the ship.

"I am?" He hadn't noticed because there were so many conflicting voices in his head.

She nodded. "What are you thinking about?"

He glanced around. A lot of people were returning to the ship at the same time as them. This wasn't the place for a serious talk. But they had to talk. He couldn't let things spiral further out of control.

"I was thinking that I'm almost out of time to tell my grandfather what is going on with his business."

"And that's all?" She arched a fine brow.

"I didn't know you were the suspicious type." He sent her a teasing smile.

"Suspicious, huh?"

They kept walking and he kept the conversation light, which was the exact opposite of how he was feeling at the moment. And somewhere along the way, Stasia had slipped her hand in his. It felt so natural for their fingers to be entwined that it drove home the reason they had to talk.

Stasia wanted more from this relationship than he could give her. He wasn't the right man for her. He didn't know how to have a long-term relationship. His parents were terrible role models. And he was a workaholic. Not exactly the criteria for a faithful, devoted companion.

When they reached Stasia's cabin, she opened the door and stepped inside. He paused at the doorway, not sure he trusted himself to go any farther. All his good intentions were likely to go out the window if she were to turn those big brown eyes on him. He would be putty in her hands, but he couldn't let her see his weakness because in the end, this thing between them, it wasn't real.

"Aren't you coming in?" she asked.

He shook his head. "I can't stay."

"Of course. You need to get back to work—"

"Stasia, it's not that." Although he did need to find the answer for his grandfather—prove that he was the rightful heir to the Carrass dynasty. But first he had to put right what he'd broken. "We need to talk."

The smile faded from her face. "It sounds serious."

"It is." He wasn't sure where to begin. "I owe you an apology."

Her brows rose. "For what?"

"The other night." He raked his fingers through his hair, scattering the short strands. He searched for the right words.

"The other night was what?"

There was no way to sugarcoat this. His gaze lowered because he just couldn't stand to see the pain that would be reflected in her eyes. "It was a mistake."

"A…a mistake?" Her voice was hollow.

When he lifted his gaze, he found she'd turned her back to him. She busied herself by taking off her shoes. Every bit of him longed to go to her— to wrap his arms around her waist—to plant a kiss on the slope of her neck—to hold her in his arms until the sun came up.

Stasia was amazing. If he ever imagined falling in love and starting a family, it would be with someone like Stasia. She was kind but insightful, beautiful but down-to-earth.

She turned to him. "You were saying why this was a mistake."

He couldn't read her thoughts. Her expression was blank. This was not the reaction he had been expecting. Still, she stood there staring at him, waiting for him to speak.

"I'm sorry. I acted without thinking. It shouldn't have happened."

She crossed her arms. "You don't think we're good together?"

That was the real problem. He did think they were good together, but he couldn't tell her that. "I think I'm not the man for you. And I don't want to hurt you."

"I appreciate you trying to let me down gently, but it's not necessary."

"It's not?"

She shook her head. "I didn't think we were anything serious. We agreed to be a couple for the length of the cruise. It's only natural being so close that one thing might lead to another, but I didn't expect this—" she waved between her and him "—to last."

He breathed a sigh of relief. This was going so

much easier than he'd ever imagined. "So then we're still on track?"

She nodded. "Don't worry. Everything is good."

It didn't feel good. His gaze met hers and he still wasn't able to get a handle on her feelings. "Then I'll go."

"I'll freshen up and then I'll meet you at your cabin."

Really? This seemed too good to be true. "Are you sure you want to do that?"

She didn't say anything as though considering her choices. "I said I'd help and I will."

He pulled the door closed behind him and then started down the passageway. He'd noticed how the light in her eyes had dimmed. No matter what she said, he'd hurt her. And that was the last thing he'd meant to do.

DAY FOURTEEN

Naples, Italy

"MAYBE WE'RE GOING about this the wrong way," Roberto said.

Stasia leaned back in her chair and stretched her sore muscles. Leaning over a laptop for hours made for aches and pains. "What do you mean?"

"I mean, we're going about this with a micro view. Perhaps we should pull back and go about it with a macro view."

"But we already went over the balance sheet. It tied in to the supplemental files." She wasn't getting his meaning, but she did agree that what they were doing now wasn't working.

It didn't help that she was distracted by their earlier conversation. His words had been like nails driven into her heart. But she had no one to blame but herself. She knew from the start that this relationship was temporary.

"I don't know." Roberto's voice drew her attention. "Maybe we have to do spot checks on the expenses because if there's going to be something unscrupulous, it's going to be with the outgoing funds. Let's hope we get lucky."

"Spot checks? You mean like pick a random number—"

"Or entry. And track it back to its origin."

She could feel his rising desperation. The cruise was over in less than two days and he so desperately wanted to have the answers for his grandfather. And she wanted to help him find those answers. But was this really the right way to go about it?

His fingers were already moving over the keyboard when she said, "Isn't this like throwing a dart at a board and just hoping it hits the bull's-eye?"

Roberto paused and glanced up at her. "If this business were smaller. If the numbers didn't run in the hundreds of millions, then yes, I would agree with you, but we just don't have time to do a full-fledged audit. My grandfather wants answers now."

"And you want to show him that you're the man to give him those answers."

His gaze met hers, but he didn't say the obvious.

After a few minutes, he said, "Okay. I've just printed off a couple of pages of entries. Pick a few numbers on each sheet and trace them back to their invoices."

"Invoices? We don't have that sort of detail."

"No. But I have the password and access to the company's servers. We'll be able to pull everything, as the system is automated and all the invoices are stored digitally."

And so they set to work. Time passed quickly with few results because it was a big task. They started with a vendor and then tracked the payments back through the system.

The first number was tracked back to a legitimate invoice.

The second tracked back accordingly.

The third and the fourth did, as well.

Stasia was beginning to think this was a fruitless mission. And the hour was getting late. Dinner had been a number of hours ago and she was starting to get tired as well as hungry.

As though he sensed her restlessness, Roberto glanced up from his laptop. "You should call it a night."

The idea was so tempting. This was the last

place she wanted to find herself. Being so close to Roberto and yet so far apart was excruciating. But she'd told him that she would help him find answers and she wasn't going back on her word.

Her gaze met his. "What about you? Do you want to get some sleep and tackle it again tomorrow?"

He shook his head. "I want to get through a few more numbers."

She restrained a sigh. "That's what I was thinking too."

He arched a disbelieving brow. "Are you sure? I'd totally understand if you want to go."

She shook her head. "But can we call for food? I'm starved."

He smiled. "I like the way you think."

They continued to work, verifying number after number. Then something didn't quite add up. Stasia had an expenditure on the reports that tied to an invoice. When she took it a step further, she could not locate a company that went by the name on the invoice.

Knock. Knock.

Stasia was so confused. She refused to give up until she resolved this mysterious company. Because there was a lot of money charged off to it over the years for construction materials.

"I'll get the door," Roberto said.

She didn't say anything as she was caught up in what she was reading on the internet. The company name did not have a website that she could find, and in this day and age of technology, that threw up a red flag for her. And then she typed in the phone number from the invoice. It said it belonged to a woman by a totally different name.

Roberto closed the door and set the food on the nightstand next to his bed since they had the table covered with their computers and papers. "I thought you were hungry."

"I, uh…" She typed in the physical address listed on the invoice.

Roberto moved to her side. "You what? Did you find something?"

"I don't know." Using online global mapping, she tracked the address down to an empty lot. "This invoice, it's not making sense."

He crouched down next to her. "You mean the amount isn't matching up?"

She shook her head. "It matches. But I decided to go a step further with each invoice and check out the company. This particular company, I don't think it's legit."

"Do you mind?" He gestured to the computer.

"Look for yourself. Maybe I'm more tired than I thought."

He swung the laptop around and started moving through the various reports that were all open on the screen. He repeated all her steps, from doing an internet search for the company name to the phone number and the physical address. All were the same results.

Then he asked to borrow her phone.

"What are you doing?" she asked.

"I'm calling the number." His finger moved over the screen.

"But it's late."

"And this is too important to wait around." He pressed a button and put the phone on Speaker.

It rang a few times, and just about the time that Stasia thought no one was going to answer, a female voice came on the line. Roberto asked if this was the company name on the invoice. The woman said it wasn't. He asked if she'd ever heard of the company. She said she hadn't and asked who he was and what he wanted. The woman was very nice, but she was no help as far as finding the company.

After Roberto disconnected the phone call, he dialed again. This time turning off the speaker-phone.

"Who are you calling now?"

He held up a finger as he pressed the phone to his ear this time. "Grandfather, I hope I didn't wake you."

Roberto asked him if he had ever heard of the company. They continued to speak for a few minutes, after which Roberto told him he wasn't prepared to report anything on his findings just yet.

After Roberto disconnected the call, she looked at him. "Well…"

"My grandfather said there used to be a company by that name, but they'd gone out of business a number of years ago."

"Which explains why they don't have an internet presence. So then why is your grandfather's business still paying them?"

"That's what I intend to find out."

"But first food." She got to her feet and led him to the food. "Eat," she said in a firm tone.

Roberto's brows lifted. "Has anyone ever told you that you're bossy?"

"If you're trying to charm me—"

"You think being called bossy is charming?"

She thought about it for a minute. "Sure. I like being taken seriously."

"Oh, I take you seriously. Especially when you uncover what is surely a case of embezzlement." He stepped closer to her. "This is it. My grandfather will at last take me seriously and offer me the CEO position."

"It's your birthright. Of course he will."

Roberto shook his head. "You don't know my grandfather. It's his way or no way. But this revelation changes things. This is exactly what I needed. Do you have any idea how amazing you are?"

"Stop." She couldn't have him flirting with her. It was too painful. He had his answer. Her job was finished. "I have to go."

She turned and headed for the door.

"Stasia. Wait."

She kept going. If she were to stop now—if she were to look into his eyes—her bravado would crumble. And she refused to make a fool of herself in front of him by letting him know that she'd fallen for her pretend fiancé.

DAY FIFTEEN

Rome, Italy

THE CRUISE WAS almost over.

And she'd concentrated on everyone but herself.

Stasia realized that was a pattern she'd developed in her life. First, it was Lukos. She'd given up her dream of a career in order to follow his career. And after she lost Lukos, she let Xander have a say in her future. Even on this cruise, she'd let Roberto distract her from her goals. It had to stop.

Stasia had stayed in her cabin that morning, not venturing on the tour of Rome and all its many splendors. She didn't have any other excuses—any other distractions.

Everything was taken care of with Roberto. His project for his grandfather was complete. And he was about to step into his birthright. She couldn't be happier for him.

She would miss him. More than she'd ever imagined possible. Her heart ached at just the thought of not seeing Roberto every day. And even worse, she could imagine him avoiding her at every turn after the way things on this cruise got way more involved than either of them planned.

She sighed. Worrying about the future wasn't going to help anything. The best thing she could do was to make a final decision on her future.

At last she knew what she wanted—a chance to help people. It fulfilled her. It gave her a purpose. And it would help so many others.

She didn't have to think any further. She knew what to do. But now she needed to take action—put motion behind her words.

Stasia grabbed her phone. She looked up the email correspondence from the woman at the hospital where Lukos had been treated and she placed the call. When she told the woman she would like to expand on their services and create a foundation, the woman promised to do everything she could to help smooth the way.

By the time Stasia hung up, she was smiling. This foundation would carry her late husband's name. It seemed so fitting and she hoped Lukos would be proud of her efforts.

For so long she'd told herself she'd secluded herself because she had to figure out her life's path, but the truth was she wanted a chance to lick her wounds—her deep wounds. And they hadn't gone away, but they were healing now. The scars would always linger but they were now a part of her, just like Lukos would always be a part of her. She would never be the woman she used to be, but she hoped she would be a better person for having known and loved Lukos.

Now she was ready to start life once again.

And she'd foolishly thought she'd found the right person to share it with.

And she'd been totally wrong.

She might have said all the right things to Roberto when he'd declared their night together a mistake. A mistake? Really?

Because it'd felt like anything but a mistake. He'd been so passionate, so thoughtful, so giving. It was like the wall between them had fallen away and it was just the two of them on even ground.

She'd thought it had been the beginning of something real for them. She glanced down at the diamond ring on her finger. It felt so heavy. She slipped it off and placed it on the table next to her laptop.

She'd known what the deal was when she'd agreed to play his fake fiancée. Why should she think that would change? Her heart cried out: because it was what she'd wanted. Each day she'd spent with Roberto, they'd grown closer and she'd found out that he wasn't the shallow playboy that she'd initially thought him to be.

He was so different—so much deeper—than she'd ever imagined. But there was one thing that hadn't changed—his determination to remain a bachelor. His grandmother couldn't change his mind. The flood of vivacious single women on the ship couldn't change his mind. And she couldn't change his mind.

She had to accept that he knew what was best for his life. And it didn't include her—

Knock. Knock. Knock.

"Stasia? Are you in there?"

It was Roberto. She had thought he'd be off sharing the information they'd uncovered with his grandfather. She didn't want to see him again.

Knock. Knock.

"Stasia," he yelled. "I'm not leaving until we talk."

She jumped to her feet and rushed to the door. "Roberto, keep it down." She glanced around to see if he'd disturbed any of her neighbors. She didn't see anyone in the passageway. "Come inside." Once he was inside, she closed the door. "What are you doing here?"

His brows rose. "Am I supposed to be somewhere else?"

"I thought you'd be with your grandfather. You know, to go over things."

"My grandfather and I are getting together this evening. My grandmother dragged him off to Rome and she wouldn't take no for an answer."

"I can definitely see your grandmother doing that. She's a very determined lady."

"Looks like you've been busy." He moved to the table. "What are you doing?"

"Working on my five-year plan."

"Anything I can do to help?"

She shook her head. "Not at this point. I'm finally getting started with the foundation."

He approached her. "And that's my fault."

"Why would that be your fault?"

"Because I kept you busy worrying about my

life and my problems." He gazed into her eyes. "And I haven't thanked you nearly enough."

She shook her head. "You don't have to thank me."

"I disagree."

Knock. Knock. Knock.

Stasia ran a hand over her hair. "If I knew I was going to have this much company, I would have gotten dressed up."

She moved to the door and opened it to find one of the ship's crew standing there with a cart. What in the world?

"I'm afraid you have the wrong cabin," she said. "I didn't order food."

Roberto rushed to her side. "Actually, you do have the right place."

Stasia stepped aside while Roberto opened the door wide for the cart. And then he rushed to the table and cleared it so the man could set up what appeared to be two covered plates, a bottle of bubbly on ice and a dozen red roses. What was this man up to?

Once the table was set and the man was gone, Stasia turned to Roberto. "What are you up to?"

"Isn't it obvious? You need lunch and I need lunch. So I thought we would eat together." He approached her. "What do you say? Shall we eat?"

"Roberto—" she shook her head "—this isn't a good idea."

He held up the diamond ring. "Does it have something to do with this sitting on the table instead of being on your finger?"

Her gaze moved to the ring that twinkled at her, but she made no move to take it. "The cruise is almost over. You need to take it back."

"And I've done a lot of thinking. What would you say if I said I didn't want this to end?"

"What? But you just got done telling me that this was only temporary—a show for your grandparents."

He reached out to her. His hands gently gripped her upper arms. "I made a mistake. You and I, we make a great team. If my grandfather offers me the CEO position, which I think was his motive behind this project, it'll mean moving to Alexandroupoli. We can start a life there."

Her head was spinning. A life with Roberto? He was saying all the right things except for the *L* word. And there was no way she would plan a future with someone who couldn't say he loved her.

Wait. He said that he was moving. Alexandroupoli was quite a way from Athens. And she'd just made a commitment to start her foundation in Athens. It'd taken her a long time to figure out just the right thing to do with her life and this felt right. She couldn't—she wouldn't give it up. She had to break the pattern.

And there was the crux of the problem. Everyone wanted something from her. His family wanted her to marry Roberto. He wanted her to give up everything to follow his dreams.

She couldn't do it. She couldn't give up on herself again. She needed this foundation. She needed to know that she could do it. She needed to know that she could stand on her own two feet and follow through with her dream.

"Roberto, I said I'd be your fiancée for the length of the cruise. Not any longer than that."

He stared at her for a moment. "I didn't mean for you to continue being my fake fiancée. I want you to be there with me, by my side, in a real relationship."

Her gaze searched his. There was nothing about love. He didn't feel the same for her.

"I can't do that. I'm staying in Athens. I'm

starting the foundation. It's something I need to do on my own."

His expression hardened. "And what about us?"

"There is no us." The words tore at her heart, but she knew in the long run that it was for the best. Roberto was not a man to be tied down. "We got caught up in the charade. It's over now. We have to go back to reality. Alone. It's the only way."

His eyes grew darker as a muscle in his cheek twitched. He surely couldn't be mad that she'd beat him to the punch. He couldn't actually think they'd last. Did he?

"I should go." And with that, he stormed out the door, closing it with a solid thud.

DAY SIXTEEN

Athens, Greece

TODAY WAS THE end of their cruise.

The end of their engagement. The end of seeing her every single day.

He'd been up all night. Every time he'd closed his eyes, Stasia's image came to mind. And he couldn't forget her final words to him. They'd been sharp and had cut right through him.

Early that morning, he'd meandered to the deck, where he'd watched the sun rise. Though it should have filled him with some sort of joy, it had done nothing for him. The brilliant colors of the sunrise were like a taunt to his gray mood.

"Roberto?"

He inwardly groaned. The last person he wanted to talk to was his grandmother.

"Roberto, what are you doing out here?" His grandmother stopped at his table and looked at him with confusion reflected in her eyes. "Shouldn't you be packing?"

"I already did it." He didn't want to talk. He just wanted to sit here alone with his thoughts.

Yaya glanced around. "Where's Stasia?"

He shrugged, looking down at his lap, where he was holding the engagement ring. "I don't know."

She sat down. "Roberto, what's wrong?"

He sighed. "It's over. It's all over."

"What is? I don't understand."

He started at the beginning, telling his grandmother about the charade and how it somehow became real—or at least he thought it had turned into a real relationship. Obviously, he'd been mistaken.

He handed her the engagement ring. "You need to take this back."

Yaya accepted the ring. She stared at it a moment. "Are you sure about this?"

"Positive. She dumped me." The acknowledgment was like an arrow through his heart.

"And that's it? You're just going to let her walk away?"

He frowned at his grandmother. "You want me to go back so she can do it again?"

Yaya shook her head. "That's not what I meant." She reached out and placed a hand on his arm. "I know that this isn't the first time you've been dumped. That was the exact word you used when your parents left you with us—"

"I don't want to talk about them. This has nothing to do with them."

"But I think it does. What your parents did was wrong and they hurt you deeply. You learned how to protect yourself by keeping others out. And you stopped telling people how you feel."

He turned to her. "What are you saying? That I'm the reason Stasia dumped me?"

"I just want you to think about it. Did you give her a reason to stay? Did you tell her that you love her—really love her?" His grandmother looked at the ring and then placed it back in his hand. "You hang on to this a while longer. I have a feeling you might need it." His grandmother stood. "Now I'm off to find some more bags. I've bought more things than I thought. Your grandfather is having a fit because there's no room in the luggage."

Roberto didn't hear his grandmother leave. He was too busy considering what she'd told him. Was she right? Had he been holding himself back?

Would Stasia feel different about him if he told her the truth? Just the thought of baring his deepest feelings to her with the chance that she'd reject him—much like his parents had rejected him when he'd begged them not to leave—left him feeling more vulnerable than he ever had in his whole life. Could he do it?

Ending things with Roberto was one of the hardest things she'd ever had to do.

Stasia had cried herself to sleep. And now in the morning light, her face was still puffy and her head hurt, but not as much as her heart.

As she exited the ship, her feet felt as though they were weighted down. Each step she took away from the ship—away from Roberto—was like another piece of her heart being torn away. What was she doing? Why was she walking away from him?

She'd been telling herself that Roberto didn't love her, but would a man who didn't care about her put a family heirloom on her finger? She had to admit that was pretty extreme even for a fake fiancée.

And then there was the way he'd spoiled her on her birthday, making her feel like a princess. And the way he'd talked with her about her future. And then there was their lovemaking. It had been so gentle and giving. That most definitely hadn't just been sex. It had been the closest she'd ever been to a person—heart, body and soul.

She glanced over her shoulder as though Roberto would be standing there. He wasn't. Was it possible she was remembering what she wanted to?

"Stasia?"

She turned her head forward, finding her brother standing there. "Xander, what are you doing here?"

"Looks like I'm just in time." He came to a stop in front of her. "Why are you crying?"

She touched her cheek, finding it damp. She hadn't even realized the tears had slipped down her cheeks. She rubbed at her face. "It doesn't matter."

"It's a guy, isn't it?"

She couldn't deny it.

"Stasia, what's going on?" Xander looked at her with concern reflected in his eyes. "Who upset you?"

Maybe if she'd been more willing to be honest with herself, with Roberto and with her brother about her feelings, she wouldn't feel so terrible now. This was supposed to be her chance to turn over a new leaf in her life. She would start with the truth.

She leveled her shoulders and lifted her chin. "Xander, there's something I need to tell you."

"Okay. I'm listening."

"I've made a decision. I'm not going into business with you." Disappointment reflected in his eyes but she didn't let that stop her. "I'm sorry. I know you've tried to include me and I really appreciate all you've done. But I have to follow my heart."

He arched a brow. "Follow your heart, doing what?"

"I'm going to start a foundation to help support the families of cancer patients. There are so many programs for the ill, but there's not a lot for the caregivers. I want to do something to support them so they can give their all to their ill loved ones." She paused. Her breath caught in her throat as she waited to hear what her brother thought of her plans.

"I think that's a great idea. When you're ready,

let me know and I'll donate or do whatever you need."

A smile pulled at her lips. "Thank you."

"But that still doesn't explain what had you so upset when I first saw you." His gaze searched hers. "If some guy has hurt you, tell me. I'll take care of him."

She glanced away, finding Roberto standing on the deck of the ship speaking to his grandfather. She'd love to know what was being said. She hoped there would be peace between the two men.

She turned her attention back to her brother. She was on a roll. She might as well keep going. "Xander, thank you for being there after Lukos passed. I really needed you, but I need you to understand that I have to figure things out on my own. I need to be able to make my own decisions without you watching over my shoulder and without worrying you'll be disappointed with my actions."

"You never disappoint me." He rubbed the back of his neck. "I just worry about you. I don't want you to be hurt again."

"But I will be and you have to be okay with that. I don't want to live in a glass house where no one can reach me and where I don't feel anything. I want to takes chances and live life to its fullest."

Her thoughts circled back to Roberto. If she were going to take chances, it should be with him. If she were going to live life to the fullest, it should be with him. So why exactly was she walking away from the man she loved without asking if he felt the same way about her?

Her gaze met her brother's. "I've got to go. I have something to do."

She turned and rushed off in the direction of the ship. She heard her brother call to her but she didn't care. She had to do this. She had to take this chance.

As she drew closer to Roberto and his grandfather, she overheard his grandfather say, "You strike a tough bargain, but I think we can make this work." His grandfather held out his hand to him. "Welcome back to the company."

Roberto shook his hand, all the while smiling.

Stasia came to a halt. Roberto was smiling. He was happy. Maybe it would be best just to leave well enough alone.

"Stasia—" her brother's voice came from behind her "—what's going on?"

It was then that Roberto and his grandfather noticed her standing off to the side. Roberto's gaze caught and held hers. Her heart pounded in her chest. She should say something, but no words came to mind.

Xander stepped forward. His gaze moved between her and Roberto. "It's him?"

Stasia was done keeping secrets. She nodded.

Xander's expression hardened. He moved toward Roberto in determined steps. "You were supposed to watch over her—keep her from getting hurt."

Stasia rushed to stand between the two most important men in her life. "Xander, I love you. But this is none of your business."

"I can explain," Roberto said.

"We don't want to hear it." Xander pressed his fists to his sides with a glare written all over his face. "You screwed up. Big-time."

"Ignore him," Stasia said to Roberto. "I want to hear what you have to say."

Just then Roberto's grandmother joined them. "What's going on?"

"Shh…" Roberto's grandfather said. "You don't want to miss this."

Roberto approached Xander. "First, Xander,

I resign. I'm sorry for the short notice, but with you moving most of the operations to Infinity Island, this is probably the best time for a change."

When Xander went to say something, Stasia glared at him and he closed his mouth without saying a word. She didn't want her brother to ruin one of his closest friendships.

"And second—" Roberto moved to stand directly in front of her "—thanks to your support, I am taking the CEO position. However, my grandfather and I have hammered out a deal where the headquarters are to be moved to Athens."

"Really?" A big smile pulled at her lips. The thought of Roberto being close by, the thought of being able to see him regularly, almost offset the sadness of calling off their engagement. "But I don't understand. Why would you do that?"

"You honestly don't know?" When she shook her head, he said, "Because I love you. I love the way you smile. I love your laugh. I love your generous heart. I love everything about you. I'm sorry I didn't tell you sooner, but someone set me straight." He glanced at his grandmother, who had happy tears in her eyes. Roberto turned his attention back to Stasia. "And I plan to stick around until you realize that you love me too."

Her heart swelled. "You won't have to wait long because I already love you."

A smile lit up Roberto's face as he pulled her into an embrace and kissed her. The kiss was short but it left no doubt in her mind that there would be more to follow soon.

When he pulled back, he said, "I think I have something that belongs to you." He pulled the engagement ring from his pocket. He bent down on one knee.

Her heart lodged in her throat. She had never expected this. His gaze held hers. When her gaze blurred from happy tears, she blinked repeatedly.

"I know I did this once before, but I want to do it over again, the right way." He took her hand in his and held the ring at the end of her finger. "Stasia, you've shown me what true love is. You've shown me that some risks are worth taking. I want us to walk through life side by side with no one in the lead. If you give me the chance, I'll be your biggest cheerleader. I believe you're capable of anything you set your mind to." He stared deep into her eyes. "Stasia, I love you with all my heart. Will you be my partner in life?"

"Yes. Oh, yes." Happy tears splashed onto her cheeks as he slid the ring on her finger.

After Roberto stood and kissed her again, they turned to Xander, waiting for his reaction.

"What's everyone looking at me for?" Xander's stony expression burst into a big smile. "I couldn't be happier for either of you." He hugged each of them.

And then Roberto's grandparents stepped forward. She'd forgotten they were still there. A puzzled expression was written over his grandfather's face. "I don't understand. I thought you were already engaged."

Everyone started to laugh. Roberto promised to fill his grandfather in later, but right now he had plans with his fiancée. They had wedding plans to make because August wasn't that far off.

EPILOGUE

August... Infinity Island, Greece

THEY'D PASSED THE TEST.

Stasia smiled. Not that she ever had any doubt about their compatibility. Still, not everyone passed the wedding test issued by Infinity Island. They were meant to be.

She stood in what used to be Popi's bungalow. But now that she had married the love of her life, Apollo, and moved to the Drakos estate, where she had started her own wedding business, this bungalow had been designated the bridal suite. It was where the brides came and stayed until the big day.

Stasia had been here for a week. Not only did she want to take part in the wedding preparations, but she also wanted to spend some time with her family before Roberto swept her off on a monthlong honeymoon in Alaska, of all places. He said they had sun and sand whenever they wanted, but snowy peaks and cozy fires were for snuggling. She had a distinct impression that they'd be doing a lot more than snuggling in the luxury cabin that he'd reserved for them.

Roberto had been tying things up at the office all week and she couldn't wait to see him. Now that he had taken over the family business, he had been working long hours to undo the damage the former accounts manager had done. The authorities had arrested the man and were still working on tracking down the funds that had been meticulously siphoned from the company.

But in the end, Roberto's grandfather was able to retire in peace. He knew the company was in good hands. And with the safeguards Roberto had implemented since taking the reins, the likelihood of anything like this ever happening again had been greatly reduced.

And Roberto's grandfather was so thrilled that they were tying the knot that he had agreed to step back in and run the company while Roberto enjoyed a nice long honeymoon. Stasia was thrilled to see the two men drawn back together.

Roberto's parents, on the other hand, were coming to the wedding, separately. Though some things changed, others stayed the same. At least

Roberto had accepted that marriage and love didn't have to be as complicated as his parents' relationship with each other and with him.

Knock. Knock.

"Stasia, are you in there?"

Her heart leaped with joy. It was Roberto, at last.

She rushed to the door and swung it wide open. "You arrived just in time."

"What? Did you think I'd be late for my own wedding?"

The thought had crossed her mind. She knew how wrapped up he could get when he was working, but she also knew he could be just as devoted to his family. And that was something she loved about him, his passion for the things that mattered most to him.

"You did?" He glanced at her with an astonished look on his face. "You really thought I'd forget our big day?"

"No, of course not." When he arched a disbelieving brow, she said, "But I know how distracted you can get in your work."

"Not enough to forget you." He leaned forward and kissed her. Not a brief peck, but a long deep thorough kiss to prove to her just how much she mattered to him.

When he finally pulled away, her heart was hammering in her chest. And the news she had to share with him had somehow escaped her.

Not wanting to stay inside on such a beautiful day, she said, "Let's take a walk."

Hand in hand, they made their way to the beach. This was where their wedding was to take place. White chairs were already set up on either side of the sandy aisle that would be lined with white rose petals just before the service began.

And at the end of the aisle stood an arch draped in white tulle. It would have small blue flowers alongside white roses adorning the arch. Both Lea and Popi had come together once more to make this a very special wedding. And they had outdone themselves. It was everything Stasia had been hoping for and more.

"Do you think we should be here?" Roberto asked.

"Why not? After all, it is our wedding."

And wait until he saw the strapless dress she'd chosen for the big day. Her hair would be pulled back in a loose braid with small flowers inserted.

On her feet would be sandals with beaded lace over the tops of her feet.

Roberto smiled at her. "Does this mean you'll stop worrying now?" When she nodded, he said, "Good. Because I'm not going anywhere. And in just a couple of hours we're going to be husband and wife." He studied her face for a moment. "You still have something on your mind. What can I say to convince you that absolutely nothing is going to go wrong today?"

"I'm not worried. Honest."

"There is something on your mind—I can see it in your eyes."

And then it came back to her, the big news she had to share with him. She just hoped that he was as excited about it as she was.

"I have some stuff to discuss with you and I didn't want to do it over the phone."

His dark brows drew together in a worried line as he reached out and took her hands in his. "What is it?"

"First, the paperwork for the foundation has come through. We're all approved and everyone I invited to be on the board has accepted."

Relief eased the worry lines on his face, and in

their place, a smile lifted his lips. "That's wonderful." He leaned down and gave her a brief kiss. "I'm so proud of you. I knew you could do anything you set your mind on." He paused. "You said the first thing—that implies you have more news."

"I… I do." She gazed into his eyes, finding the added strength she needed to put the words out there. "Roberto, I have something to tell you that I hope you will find as exciting as I do."

A guarded look crossed his handsome face. "And this news, would it have anything to do with expanding our family?"

Her mouth gaped. "How…how did you know?"

A smile covered his face and lit up his eyes. "Call it wishful thinking."

"Call it whatever you want, but the doctor says in seven months and one week, we're going to be calling you Daddy."

"Woo-hoo!" He picked her up in his arms and swung her around. When he settled her feet back on the ground, he said, "I didn't think it was possible to make this day any better, but somehow you found a way. Thank you for making me see that life can be more than I ever imagined. I am truly living a dream."

"You are my dream too. I love you."

"I love you too."

* * * * *

LET'S TALK
Romance

For exclusive extracts, competitions
and special offers, find us online:

 facebook.com/millsandboon

@millsandboonuk

@millsandboon

Or get in touch on 0844 844 1351*

For all the latest titles coming soon,
visit millsandboon.co.uk/nextmonth

Want even more
ROMANCE?

Join our bookclub today!

'Mills & Boon books, the perfect way to escape for an hour or so.'

Miss W. Dyer

'Excellent service, promptly delivered and very good subscription choices.'

Miss A. Pearson

'You get fantastic special offers and the chance to get books before they hit the shops'

Mrs V. Hall

Visit millsandbook.co.uk/Bookclub and save on brand new books.

MILLS & BOON